DOG MEAT

Priscilla Bettis

Potter's Grove Press 2022

Cover art by **Jaganath Venaka**

This book is a work of fiction. Names, characters, places, and incidents either are products of the author's imagination or are used fictitiously. Any resemblance to actual persons, living or dead, events, or locales is entirely coincidental.

First Printing: November 2022
Potter's Grove Press, LLC
www.pottersgrovepress.com

ISBN-13 **978-1-951840-61-7**

Please donate to the dog rescue organization of your choice.

CHAPTERS

UNU

(One)

Ward looped the noose around the mongrel's neck. The two of them, Ward and the dog, were in the courtyard behind the Yulin Dish restaurant in the northernmost city of the Colony. A chin-high concrete wall enclosed the courtyard, and shards of glass were embedded upright in the top of the wall.

Some of the dogs whined from the back corners of their chain-link cages. Others lay on their concrete pads, panting in the September afternoon heat. Beyond the wall, columns of cinderblock boxes stacked one atop another rose and pierced the smoggy sky. Ward eyed the middle column. Third floor, third window from the right, his concrete box, his apartment.

Ward dropped the loose end of the noose and let the mongrel wander freely. It was easier to get the nooses on when none of the dogs were in distress. He double-checked to make sure the bamboo pole, sullied with dried bodily fluids and shriveled fleshy bits, was on the other side of the courtyard so it wouldn't alarm the dogs.

He skipped the husky because huskies had a thick under-fur, a natural cushioning. They were difficult to kill. He opened the next cage. A trembling spaniel slunk past Ward's legs.

His right arm buzzed. It always started that way. The thinking, self-aware part of his brain would escape through his skin, seeping first through the pale surface of his forearm, then his shoulder, then eventually the rest of his body. He didn't understand how he could perform his work and yet see himself, from outside his body, working. He shook his head. *Something only the ancestors understand.*

Back near the cages, the mongrel sat and pawed at the noose. Her underside was exposed, and her teats were swollen.

"Do your pups miss their mother?" Ward asked the mongrel. He didn't see his own mother often enough, but it must be worse for puppies who depend on their mother for nourishment. The dog caught her paws in the noose and ineffectively spun it around her neck. Soon she would figure out how to push it off her head instead. Ward would have to hurry.

Just when he got the rope secured around the spaniel, Ward's boss, Fay, stuck her head out the back door of the restaurant.

"Ward," Fay said, "tri." She held up her thumb and her first two fingers indicating *three.*

Yulin Dish specialized in dog meat. Ward would have to slaughter three dogs today, not two. A sour taste that had been building at the back of his throat flooded his mouth, and he spat. Lately, the sourness stayed with him for hours, eating away at his mouth and throat long after work was over and he had returned to his apartment.

He grabbed a third noose and opened the cage in the corner, and a shorn male dog dashed out. The shorn dog came in only yesterday. Shorn for the heat. Someone, then, cared for this dog. Whether it was a peasant's hunting companion or a wealthy family's pet, it didn't belong at Yulin Dish. Ward crouched and held his muscled arms out as if to give a hug and called to the dog with fake cheer.

"Venu!" *Come here!*

The shorn canine trotted over, and Ward slipped a noose around its head, around someone's companion, someone's pet.

Once, Ward noosed the dogs slowly on purpose, hoping the dogs would grow leery and attack him as a pack, rip him apart, and eat him like their hunter-carnivore ancestors would have. But most of these dogs had lived their short lives in breeders' cages or on the outskirts of the city, begging scraps from humans, never learning the Ways of the Dog. The only thing his slow work had done was make the last dog skittish and hard to catch.

If the dogs did ever turn on him, it'd be a better death than theirs.

Ward's job at Yulin Dish restaurant was to kill dogs for people who had scored higher on the childhood placement exam.

The shorn dog and the mongrel bowed, spun, and tussled with each other.

Both of Ward's arms were numb now, but he could still smell feces polluting the cages and still feel his bulky legs. He wasn't totally removed from his body yet.

He opened his shirt collar. "Here!" He squatted. "I offer my throat." The two playful dogs sprinted past.

Ward stomped on the mongrel's lead the next time she dashed by, catching the rope with the heel of his boot. He secured her lead on the long, horizontal bar of the steel slaughter frame.

The slaughter frame had six clamps, but of course, Ward would only need three today. Each clamp had toothy grips that bit into the leads and would not let go until the dogs were dead. The horizontal bar was on a rocker cemented into the ground. When Ward eventually got all three dog leads clamped in place, he'd pivot the bar upwards, suspending the dogs by their nooses.

"Venu!" The shorn dog trotted up, wagging its tail. Ward clamped the lead.

By the time he got the first two dogs secured, the spaniel had backed itself into the far wall of the courtyard. When Ward approached, the trembling dog tucked its tail underneath and slunk toward the resting bamboo pole. The dog must have sensed something evil about the pole because it whimpered and dashed away from it, directly toward Ward. He snatched the dog's lead and pulled. The spaniel splayed his feet and sat back.

"I wouldn't want to go with me either," Ward said. He picked up the dog, carried it to the slaughter frame, and secured the dog's lead.

He retrieved the pole.

Ward could still discern the sour taste, but his sense of smell had faded, and his legs were no longer attached to his body. He could see the top of his own head and his dark, straight hair.

One of the ancestral lessons he had learned at his mother's side as they knelt before their family shrine was *The fate of one's present existence lies in one's past existence.* Did that mean in a past life he lived in such a way as to doom himself to this life of slaughtering dogs?

The shorn dog stood proud, a dog on a leash awaiting a command. The mongrel snarled and twisted itself about, trying to snap at the lead, but the more she struggled, the tighter she made her own noose. Air hissed in and out of her constricted windpipe. The spaniel whimpered.

Another day when young Ward and his mother knelt before the ancestral shrine, she lit an extra stick of incense before the Great Hornet icon. Smaller images of butterflies, blue-tinged mountains, and human figures surrounded the Great Hornet.

"Liston to what the Great Hornet teaches, Son," she said. "The butterfly is weak in the wind and easily thrown off course." She pointed to one of the human figures on the icon. "A human must only lean into the wind to continue his path."

"What if the wind is strong?" he had asked his mother. "What if it's a typhoon?"

Ward lifted the horizontal bar of the slaughter frame and locked it in place. The dogs dangled from their nooses, and all three dogs frantically pawed the air. Even the shorn dog lost its composure and bucked. Ward was now merely an observer of his own corporeal body. His physical self grasped the bamboo pole.

And then threw it on the ground.

What if he could simply lean toward a new fate like a man trekking into the wind? Why couldn't he? After all, it wasn't he who had a rope around his neck. He unlatched the horizontal bar and lowered the dogs to the ground. After a glance at the glass-topped wall, Ward figured out his next move, but he had to work quickly before his hands regained feeling. He released each dog from its noose, and then he sprinted straight toward the wall.

"Kalb Ward!" It was the freckle-faced restaurant cadre. "Halti!" *Stop!* She had short legs but an athletic build. Her rapid footsteps fell in behind Ward's.

Ward knew the cadre was not tall enough to scale the wall. He thought he could get away if he could get his feet up and out of her reach, but if she grabbed his heel with those mannish hands of hers . . .

He sprang and planted his hands on top of the wall.

The three dogs barked, and their companions in the cages yipped.

Jagged glass sliced into Ward's palms, but it didn't hurt. All he could sense was the grip the glass provided. He used his momentum to send his body up and over. When he landed with an explosion of dust in an alleyway on the other side of the wall, his mind slammed back into his body. Pain seared his hands, and he fought to keep from crying out.

Ward grasped at the broken thoughts tumbling through his head. What exactly did he want to accomplish? He wanted to escape the cadre, yes, but more than that. He wanted to escape his monstrous self, be liberated from his life's path that fueled his nightmares. No dogs, no bamboo poles, no blood, no struggling screams. People think dogs can't scream. Most people in the city had never even seen a dog, so how would they know?

Even as the pain in his hands made his eyes water, Ward let go a mad laugh. For now, he had the freedom to go where he pleased. Whether he ran left or right was up to him.

"Halti, Ward!" the cadre yelled from the other side of the wall. "You are not allowed to . . ." Her voice trailed off. She was probably going through the butchering room and out the side door, and she'd be after him soon. No doubt she'd also be calling for help on her two-way radio.

Ward had to think fast.

He chose left. He navigated a tangle of black bicycles and sprinted past couples spending Saturday afternoon together. He wove through clusters of people all dressed for the heat in lightweight cotton pants and white, button-front shirts. No blue uniform shirts, that was good. He ran parallel to the small repair shops that fronted the alley.

A quick glance over his shoulder revealed a backstreet crowded with pedestrians, all with dark hair and pale skin, no sign of the athletic cadre. Centuries of isolation and current aesthetic norms left the Colonists with little variation in appearance, although the mountain villagers had a different facial structure, and some Colonists, like the restaurant cadre, were freckled.

A flash of a chambray blue shirt.

The cadre was catching up to Ward already. *So fast for such a short woman.* He picked up his speed.

His hands dripped blood as he scurried along the storefronts then took an abrupt turn down an even narrower alley between a row of corrugated metal shacks on one side and produce stands on the other.

He looked over his shoulder and didn't see the cadre. It gave him a chance to pause and breathe and figure out where he should go next.

His mother's apartment? No. When he became an adult, their different stations in life dictated that they wouldn't spend much time together, and never at her apartment.

Between a stack of watermelons and a crate of yellow squash, an elderly woman sat on the alleyway concrete. She wore faded silks, and her ears were snipped into slender points, or "bat ears," in honor of the Bat Gods that royalty used to worship, back when there was a royal class, back when the Bat God superstition was legal.

She held a pottery bowl in her lap. In her bowl were pieces of charred, fake money and a stick of incense. An illegal ancestral shrine.

Faded silks and snipped ears meant she had come of age during the pre-Revolution dynasty and that she and her family were members of the court—dignitaries or advisors of some kind. She would have had servants in the house. All the women would have had snipped ears and all the men shaved heads.

Blood from Ward's hands splashed on the woman's bare, arthritic feet. He tucked his hands under his armpits.

The old woman was praying and moving her gnarled hands in small circles through the smoke rising from the incense. How had she survived the Civil Revolution? Perhaps the ancestors she was praying to had protected her.

Behind the watermelon cart, a young vendor was eating a bowl of sticky rice. He pointed his fork at Ward. "You buy or you go."

Ward looked up and down the narrow alley. The cadre hadn't found him yet. The praying woman was pretty well hidden between the vendor carts. Maybe Ward could likewise hide here.

She turned her face up at Ward. One of her eyes was missing. The eyebrow over the remaining eye lifted, and she pulled aside the embroidered flap of her silk top to reveal a collection box. She was a beggar as well as a survivor of the old dynasty.

If Ward stayed here, the cadre chasing him might discover the snipped-ear beggar. This was 1986 after all, and in the Modern Colony, there were no beggars because everybody had a job. Ward could cite the tenet from memory. *Everybody has a job. Every job is important.* Ward wasn't sure what that meant for the elderly, but he left the old woman in peace and headed for the railroad tunnel.

* * *

After more than an hour of slinking through back alleys and creeping under shadowed awnings, Ward could tell he was getting close to the tunnel when he smelled hot polyamides from the sock factory. The stretch of tracks near the factory sunk below street level before burrowing under a truck bridge. No one else ever went to the tunnel as far as Ward knew. It was quiet and private, a rarity in a city this big.

Sickly alder trees that never grew beyond bush-height closed in on each side of the tracks. Coal dust choked the alders' wilting leaves and turned them black. If Ward stood near the rails and looked into the tunnel and squinted, he could just make out a spot of late afternoon daylight where the tracks exited on the far side. On a windy day, the air sprinted headlong toward the spot of light and howled like a pack of dogs.

Ward knew this bridge well. Patro, *Father*, had worked on its design. Patro didn't see it to completion before his cortisol-flooded and cane-thrashed body succumbed to a slow, withering death, a death that began the day four soldiers broke down the Ward family's door.

But the Civil Revolution was a necessary step in the destined modernization of the Colony, Ward thought, reminding himself of a civics lesson from elementary school.

A truck going too fast thundered over the bridge on its way to the sock factory.

Sometimes, when he was alone in his apartment and his door was closed and his window shut tight, he wondered what he truly believed about the Revolution. The Colony, so modern . . . his father, so damaged.

He stepped between the rails.

Walking with even strides on the cross ties, Ward descended to the overgrown, brushy section just before the tunnel. The sunlight was fading fast. Blood had stopped flowing from his cuts, and scabs were forming. In the failing light, the scabs looked as black as the sickly alder leaves.

He lay across the tracks. One rail was like the cradle of a guillotine, the other like an open shackle holding his ankles. The rails were surprisingly cold in the early evening heat. Brittle, sharp-edged cinders bit into his back, and it reminded him of the glass on top of the wall.

A vibration built up in the rail under his neck. Two hundred thousand kilograms of coal-powered muscle would sever Ward's head from his torso, and his feet from his legs. If he simply remained shackled to the guillotine, his death would last half a second. He allowed himself a small smile. No more killing dogs.

He sat up with a sigh. Less than a second was too quick and too merciful for him. The truth was, Ward had wandered many times to the tracks after the restaurant closed for the night. In his work clothes soiled with canine blood, he'd lie down and imagine a train ending his life in a violent instant. Each time, he'd decide death by train was too good and too quick.

Ward got up, and the sudden blood flow to his injured palms made his hands flare with pain. He stood for a moment and savored the sensation before trudging toward home.

* * *

As he approached his apartment building, he expected soldiers to call his name, to arrest him, but even the apartment's night cadre casually eyed him as usual when Ward entered the building.

After three flights of stairs, he turned left down the hall. The closer he got to his neighbor Lam's apartment, where she and her eight-year-old son lived, the more it smelled like onions.

Empty thermoses waited outside each apartment door. There were four empties sitting outside Lam's apartment. They would be replaced by morning with thermoses full of freshly boiled water, safe to drink.

The sound of footsteps came from the stairwell. One person, delicate shoes, so not soldiers.

Lam emerged from the stairwell. Her whole body looked like a tired sigh, as if it'd dissolve in water or disperse in a gust of wind. In one hand she had a plastic net bag with a bottle of orange soda and what looked like packaged biscuits, but Ward wasn't sure because he'd never had the luxury of eating packaged biscuits. In the other hand, she had a stack of bundled clothes tied up with string.

She lifted the bag. "A soda for my visiting husband and some cookies for my dear son." Her eyelids were droopy.

"Are you okay?" he asked.

For a moment, her lips quivered. Then she nodded.

Ward wanted to go to Lam, relieve her of her things and carry them inside for her, but he dare not allow anyone to be in his presence when the soldiers came. Especially Lam.

She must have seen him eyeing the bundle of clothes. "I just came from my father-in-law's apartment. The poor thing is too frail now to wash his own clothes or clean his own apartment, and ever since my mother-in-law died . . ."

Ward nodded. No wonder she looked exhausted.

They said their goodbyes, and Ward went inside his apartment.

He poured the rest of his boiled water, now lukewarm, on soggy tea leaves at the bottom of a glass and put his thermoses—two, because he lived alone, and two was his allotment—in the hallway. He drank his tea while waiting for his arrest.

Residents were not allowed to put locks on their doors, so Ward envisioned soldiers bursting in without warning at any minute. No one came, though, and sometime after midnight he fell asleep.

* * *

Ward woke up slumped on his desk with daylight bleeding through the window and warming the back of his neck. He hadn't wound his alarm clock. Its hands sat meaninglessly at four-thirty-five, but Ward guessed by the sun's elevation that it was late morning. If the restaurant cadre was giving him a chance to return to work today, he wouldn't take it.

His sole photograph, a picture of his parents before the Civil Revolution, sat on the corner of his desk. Patro in this photograph was broad-shouldered with a confident stance, able to feed the family with his engineering work when so much of the dynastic Colony in the 1950s and 1960s starved. Most of Ward's memories of his father, though, were of the darting-eyed man who rarely spoke and scurried like a rodent rather than walking like a human. He died when Ward was a teenager, but Patro didn't so much die as get replaced by a shadow, a shadow on the wall, a shadow on the chair. One day, even the shadow was gone, and Ward and his mother carried on with their lives.

Ward brushed his fingertip across his mother's face in the photograph. "Panjo," *Mother*, he said, "when the soldiers take me away, I will miss you." He thought for a moment about his mother's loneliness, that she would ache to see him, too. Then again, she would no longer have the shame of a son whose job was to kill dogs. She would no longer have to sneak away from her neighbors to come visit him.

He cracked his door and peeked into the hallway. It was empty. Voices from Lam's apartment let him know that her son was hungry and hadn't eaten breakfast yet. The child never missed a meal, so the apartment building's cafeteria must still be open. Ward had to empty his bladder first, and then he'd head downstairs to eat. If he got arrested on the way to breakfast, so be it.

Ward flinched when he looked down. He didn't realize he was still wearing his work boots. Each boot was laminated with layers of black, brown, and yellow organic matter splashed and dried then splashed again. There were no solitary bits that stood out from the rest. All conformed to the shape of the boot. Ward knew he was looking at the blood, viscera, and feces of hundreds of dogs. He took off his boots, set them by the door, and slipped on his yellow plastic flats.

His yellow shoes were the type that almost every adult wore whether man or woman, young adult or elderly citizen. The plastic shoes had a molded open-weave design, low heels, and rounded toes. Few citizens in the city of three million could afford leather sandals or the even more coveted American sneakers. Practically everyone wore plastic flats in pale pink or light purple. But rarely yellow. Ward slid one foot forward, turning it left then right, admiring his unique, yellow shoe. He felt like a rebel and imagined himself wearing blue jeans and meeting up in candlelit basements to read forbidden British poets or American playwrights.

But it was just a shoe, he reminded himself on the way to the bathroom. He had much bigger issues to deal with right now.

Each floor in the apartment building had a bathroom at the end of the hall, and each bathroom had four squat-style toilet stalls and one showerhead behind a plastic curtain. There was no toilet paper, that being a luxury, but there were two sinks. Ward seldom used the sinks in the bathroom because there was a sink in each apartment, and he preferred to wash his hands alone, thinking other residents were watching the canine blood run off his hands when he used the communal sinks.

"What happened?" A voice next to Ward startled him. It was Lam, and she stood close to him just inside the bathroom door.

He could tell by looking at her face that she was still exhausted, but she was neatly dressed, and her messy hair shined. As always it stuck out in clusters like wind-blown hair without the wind. He wanted to brush his fingertips through her hair, feel its silk.

She stared wide-eyed at his hands.

"I have to urinate," he said, sliding his scabbed palms into his pockets. He winced as the fabric scraped his wounds.

She pulled his hands out—something she would never have done if there had been other residents in the bathroom—and examined them.

Her touch was warm and soft like a lover's breath. She smelled as she always did of ripe, sweet onions.

"I have to urinate," he said again and pulled away. *She can't be associated with me. If they see her with me . . .*

After he finished in the bathroom, Ward brushed past Lam, ignoring her questions, and went downstairs, out the front door, and around the side of the building. He entered the squat, low-ceilinged room of the cafeteria, and his mouth watered. The cafeteria didn't serve cabbage-and-egg stir fry very often.

He waited in line while Li Ling's voice on the overhead speakers broadcast the morning news, events in the world and within the country "that are of significance to citizens of our Modern Colony." And the tenets of course, always the tenets.

13

Li Ling spoke more slowly than she did when they were children, and after years of experience as the spokeswoman for Colony Radio Morning, she enunciated like a cyber machine, perfectly. She had replaced the northwest Colony accent of their childhood, so perilously close to a peasant's way of speaking, with a more sophisticated way of speaking that walked the fence between the elite Southeast dialect and the commoners' dialect.

She and Ward had attended the same elementary school, and his heart still rushed whenever he heard her voice. He knew other men's hearts did too. The short man in the breakfast line, the way he suddenly had a faraway gaze with a hint of smile as soon as she started talking. The face of a teenager at a nearby table softened as if observing a lovely sunrise. The man over there with his rice and sweet roll who was seeking a space at a table started walking with a bounce in his step. And now a comely woman, who was likewise seeking a place to sit, the way she pulled her shoulders back and sashayed her hips as if her sexuality had been threatened and she had to compete to prove that no, a mere voice through a speaker system couldn't trump her physical allure, no matter the beauty of the voice.

Seventeen years ago, Ward and his middle school classmates had taken the government placement exam. His best friend, the beautiful Li Ling, scored high on language learning and was quickly routed to studies in phonetics, literature, and grammar. Ward had not scored high on anything and was routed to basic studies with longer physical education classes to prepare him for manual labor. No matter that he had the flu during the placement exam. No matter that his mother had an IQ of 152 and spoke three languages or that his father was a bridge engineer and an accomplished pianist.

The government had ended Ward's formal education after tenth grade.

* * *

The soldiers didn't come to Ward's apartment after breakfast. He waited until the bell tower at the east end of People's Street struck noon to reset and wind his alarm clock. Then he watched the clock's hands slowly circle for the next six hours. He couldn't understand why he hadn't been arrested yet.

That evening after dinner, he sat at his desk again and waited.

"Sweetheart, Son," Lam said, her voice drifting through the wall, "you should be in bed." The wall between apartments was only one cinderblock thick, so neighbors could easily hear one another.

"But, Pan*jooo*," came the boy's reply. The boy's voice had a childish, whiny tone, quite at odds with his humongous size. When standing, the boy came up past Ward's shoulders, and he was already wearing men's size shirts.

He's only eight, Ward reminded himself. *Eight-year-olds sometimes whine no matter how big they are.*

The proper word for *fat* in the Colonists' language escaped him. It was a rarely used word in a country that had struggled so long with famine and food rations. Then, during the Revolution, Ward had learned that to be fat like the imperialist Americans was to be ugly. *Ugly* was a word he and his fellow Colonists often substituted to describe overly fed people.

"Fat," he said the English word aloud. His mother's language lessons from when he was a boy sprang from his memories. She had taught him openly with joy when he was very young, before the Revolution. She had taught him behind closed doors with a muted voice when he was older.

"The fat pig sat on the thin stick," Ward said, remembering one of his mother's English lessons.

The soldiers did come the following morning, violently forcing their way through Ward's unlocked door. Flashlight beams swept the apartment as his broken doorknob wobbled across the floor and came to rest next to the nightstand. The glow-in-the-dark dial of Ward's alarm clock told him that it was two-thirty in the morning. Just outside his apartment, in the dimly lit hallway, Lam pointed a trembling finger at Ward. It was rude to point. That was something only the Outsiders did.

"There he is," Lam said with a scowl on her face. As soon as the last of the four soldiers passed by, she snatched her finger back, and tears flooded her eyes. She hurried away in the direction of her apartment.

DU

(Two)

The re-education camp where the soldiers took Ward was in the barrens west of the city. They arrived while it was still dark. Each guard had a number on his chest pocket rather than a name badge, and Ward quickly came to think of the men as numbers. Eleven escorted Ward past Fifty-Eight and Seventy (and their weapons) and into a prison cell. Ward's cell was a cinderblock cube, not unlike his apartment, except the cell's tiny window was wire-reinforced glass and didn't open. Also, Ward's new room had a door made of bars, and this door did have a lock.

Eleven locked Ward in his cell, and then he pointed through the bars to a pair of folded pants and matching shirt lying on a cot. "Change."

Ward stripped to his underwear. He then pulled on the pants. They were gray, lightweight cotton, and they were baggy like pajamas with a one-size-fits-all drawstring waist. The shirt was a pullover top shaped like something a toddler would wear. It was tight across Ward's muscled chest but still wearable.

The guard looked Ward up and down and nodded as if in appreciation. "We'll get a lot out of you."

"What do you mean?"

Eleven answered with a smirk, and then he sauntered off.

Ward reclined on the cot and closed his eyes. It seemed as soon as he fell asleep, a loudspeaker woke him up. Was it time to get up already? He looked up at the window. The little glass square was dark, but what choice did he have? He slipped on his yellow plastic shoes and waited, for what, he didn't know.

The loudspeaker blasted tenet after tenet. Ward cringed. It was not Li Ling's musical voice but the voice of a man who leaned too heavily on sharp consonants, as if he was yelling and running downhill at the same time.

Ward struggled to reconcile the fact that he was in prison with the belief that he'd hear Li Ling's voice again. He believed he'd *see* her again. He believed—

"Stand back!" shouted a guard before unlocking Ward's cell.

With AK-47s to encourage the prisoners' movements, guards marched Ward and the other men to the end of the hall and through the thick, metal door to an outside bathroom facility. A long, concrete trench served as a multi-user toilet, and there was a trough for washing up. Ward waited in line.

By the time it was his turn, the sooty gray smudge of smog hovering over the faraway city had turned to dirty yellow with the approaching sun. As Ward squatted and defecated, he heard high-pitched keening in the distance. The only time he heard a noise like that was from certain breeds of dogs when he first struck them with the bamboo pole. And also from his mother when Patro left with the soldiers. A women's wing, then, somewhere in another part of the camp, wives missing their husbands, mothers yearning for their children.

Ward wished he had been able to bring the photograph of his mother and father.

When Ward dunked his hands in the trough, he couldn't see his hands at all because the water was so murky. It smelled bad, too, like the restaurant courtyard before Fay hosed it down with bleach water.

As the sun fissured the horizon, guards ushered Ward and the other men aboard two Russian-made buses from the 1950s. The long, drab green vehicles headed even farther away from the city. Ward rode in the first bus with its alternately coughing and screeching engine. Fellow prisoners slept through engine noise and jolts of the worn-out suspension. Open windows did little to cool the steel oven. Besides the driver, only Ward and the two guards in the back stayed awake.

An hour later the last of the arid scrubland gave way to desert sands and granite outcrops.

A dump truck passed them going the other direction. Mounds of gravel rose above the top of the overfull dump truck and spilled onto the desolate road. Diesel fumes from the truck streamed in through the bus's windows.

The road ended in a dirt lot already full of other buses. The driver parked and turned the key, relieving the engine of its struggles. The men stepped off the bus, and a barrage of concussive sounds enveloped them. The noise was coming from out of sight down a hill, but the men turned the other direction toward a shack. The rest of the prisoners seemed to know where to go, so Ward fell in behind them. The shack was a piecemeal, tin shed that housed piles of ordinary hammers and chisels. Each man picked up one hammer and one chisel.

The tools pulled at Ward's scabs as he took hold of his set. He followed the men out of the shack and down the rocky hill.

The concussive sounds grew louder, and Ward endeavored to plug his ears while holding his tools. As the men filed past Sixty-Four, the guard laughed at Ward and gave him a shove.

Hundreds of men and women were squatting and taking hammer and chisel to big rocks and making them into little rocks. Other prisoners shoveled the little rocks into wheel barrels. One man with keloid tissue running up the side of his face had an old-fashioned, ball-and-chain fetter around his ankle. The threat of the guards' AK-47s must not have been enough to subdue the scar-faced man if he needed iron restraints, too.

Ward's mouth dropped open. He didn't know before this moment where gravel came from.

"This is very inefficient," he shouted to the nearest prisoner. Ward thought someone like his father could have designed a more efficient machine to make gravel than the slow, bang-bang of carpentry hammers.

Using his rifle, Sixty-Four prodded Ward out of his reverie and shouted something, but Ward couldn't hear the guard over the noise of an approaching front loader. Ward stepped back to get out of the way of the machine, but Sixty-Four nudged him back into place with another jab of his rifle. With a noise that rattled Ward's chest, the front loader dumped a pile of head-sized rocks not two meters away. Ward hunched in fear as the guard tossed his head back and laughed. Dust rose and obscured both men, and for a moment Ward's feet twitched with the desire to run.

Do I want to run away, so I can go back to slaughtering dogs? This has got to be better. He forced his feet to remain still. The dust fell, and the air cleared. The laughing guard coughed and pointed to the pile of large rocks as the front loader backed up.

Ward gave a slight nod. "I understand," he muttered, not caring whether or not the guard could hear him. Efficiency wasn't the point of the system. Ward squatted and placed the chisel on the rock and slammed it with the hammer. A shard of stone flew off and hit Ward in the lip. He tasted blood.

Sixty-Four laughed again.

In order to protect his teeth and eyes, Ward kept his mouth closed and lowered his lids to only a sliver of sight.

Seemingly satisfied with Ward's efforts, Sixty-Four swung his rifle over his shoulder and swaggered away.

Clouds of dust formed above the prisoners and fell and formed again. Ward's hands bled.

He put his tools down and examined his palms. He couldn't tell much for all the grit and blood, though he could see his fingers were swollen. He started to rise, and the motion caused his back to spasm since he'd been squatting for so long. Staggering first right then left, Ward finally rose to his full height and wiped his palms against one another for a closer look. Rough grains tore at his wounds and sent needles of pain across his hands. With morbid curiosity, he rubbed his hands again, harder this time, making his eyes water.

Not numbness during work, but pain. He relished the sensation.

A gaunt prisoner, an older man, shuffled over. He had inflamed bald patches on his head.

"What is it?" asked the old man.

Ward held his palms out for the man to see. A wave of sadness rose in Ward's chest when he noted the similarities between Patro's pianist hands and this man's long, probing fingers.

The older prisoner shook his head as he examined Ward's palms. "This is not from blisters." He flipped Ward's hands over and palpated the bones.

"Dok!" *Doctor!* Fifty-One yelled, brandishing his rifle as he strode toward Ward and his fellow prisoner.

The stooped man ignored or didn't hear the guard.

Ward asked, "You're a doctor?"

"I was." He had a fresh welt on the side of his neck, and one sleeve of his gray shirt had been torn away and revealed old bruises.

"I quit my job," said Ward as an explanation as to why he was at the camp.

Fifty-One was approaching fast.

"I refused to quit mine," replied the old man. "Medicine should know no borders." He leaned in. "Outsider medicine doesn't have all the answers," he said in a voice only barely loud enough to be heard with all the hammers and machinery. Pulling back, he shouted into the air, "But neither does Colony medicine!"

Ward didn't understand what the man meant but judging from the man's age (about the age Patro would have been), he assumed it had something to do with the Civil Revolution.

Fifty-One arrived and swung his rifle between the doctor and Ward. The guard knocked the doctor to the ground, ending the old man's makeshift medical examination of Ward's hands.

An image of Patro flashed in Ward's mind, and his chest tightened. It was hard to breathe. Suddenly he was a little boy again.

* * *

It was the rise of the Civil Revolution, and the Ward family's intellectualism was seen as a threat to the Revolution's success. Soldiers took Patro away by gunpoint and sledgehammer.

Ward and his mother were on their own for two years. His father returned the year of the mass cannibal rituals. Ward was nine.

Gone was the man who sang at the piano or tossed Ward in the air while making silly sounds of geese. Gone was the man who spoke with rapid gestures and broad smiles about the bridge he and the other engineers were designing. The man who returned had darting eyes and hair that hung over his face. Calluses textured his palms. Pink and white splotches colored his skin where the sun had blistered his neck and back. He was afflicted with nervoj, *bad nerves,* a condition which sent him diving to the floor with any sudden, loud sound, and he was silent except for late-night cries due to terrors that now controlled his dreams.

Eventually, Ward's father went back to his engineering job, but he often walked with his hands clutched to his chest as if hiding a secret part of himself. Whatever he was hiding, he kept it near his heart. The soldiers had taken everything else.

* * *

Rising to his feet, the old doctor pointed at Ward's hands. "You ignorant guard. His hands will get infected. He won't be able to work if you leave him like this."

Fifty-One briefly inspected Ward's hands, and his face softened. "Fix him, old man," the guard said and went back to his post by the wheelbarrows.

Shaking his head, the doctor said, "I have nothing to keep this from being infected." He turned his rheumy eyes toward Ward and cackled. "This is going to hurt like hell." He proceeded to wring blood out of Ward's wounds by squeezing first his shoulders then his forearms then his wrists. Again and again, the doctor squeezed.

Ward started to pull away.

The doctor said, in a serious tone this time, "I know it hurts, but don't lift your arms."

"I don't mind the pain, but a lot of blood is coming out."

"On purpose. You are washing your wounds." The doctor grinned, baring broken teeth. "A tough one, you. Most people would have fainted by now."

To feel rather than inflict pain. Ward smiled.

The thin doctor had surprisingly strong hands, presumably from all the gravel work he did, but still, Ward could tell the man was weakening. "Dok, is there anything I can do to help you?"

The old man grunted with effort. "Almost . . . done."

When both of Ward's hands were shiny with fresh blood and a pool of red mud lay at his feet, the doctor-prisoner instructed Ward to hold his hands over his head until scabs formed.

"Your arms will fatigue," the doctor said, "but you are tough." He shuffled back to his pile of rocks.

Ward's injured hands stopped bleeding soon after he lifted them in the air. In another twenty minutes or so, scabs formed, and Ward went over to show the doctor.

The old man nodded. "Now I'll bandage your hands." Before Ward could stop him, the doctor removed his shirt, uncovering fresh bruises over his kidneys, and tore into the cloth with his jagged teeth. Soon, Ward's hands had mitten-sized, gray bandages that held his hands in the shape of hooks.

"That way you can still hold the hammer and chisel," the doctor said. He gestured at Fifty-One. "They won't let you *not* hold a hammer and chisel. The scabs keep infectious matter out, and the bandages keep the scabs in place. Wiggle your thumbs."

Ward wiggled his thumbs.

"Good, you can still eat and take a shit." What sunlight forced its way through the dust of the gravel mine illuminated the inflamed patches of the doctor's scalp.

"What happened to your head?"

The doctor broke out in a hysterical laugh. He reached up and yanked out wisps of hair still remaining at his temple. He turned his back on Ward and shambled off to his pile of rocks.

When the old man squatted and picked up his hammer, it dawned on Ward that the doctor had been a member of the pre-Revolution royal court. *With no way to shave his head, the crazy fool is plucking it.* Despite the heat, a shiver ran up Ward's spine. *I let this mad man bleed me half dry.*

After another hour of work, big machinery sounds and diesel engine rumbles came to an abrupt halt. It was lunch. Having had no breakfast, Ward's stomach was empty and starting to cramp. Under the escort of the guards' rifles, the prisoners made their way to a tent with stacks of cold sweet rolls and boiled peanuts, food the prisoners could eat with their hands. A large image of the Colony's Chairman hung at the far side of the tent. An overhead speaker burst to life, yet again proclaiming the tenets. The speaker was almost as loud as the hammers had been, and all the noise was making Ward dizzy.

He wandered to the edge of the tent, standing as far away from the speaker as he could. His plastic shoes had filled with grit and were rubbing his feet, but he was glad he wasn't back at the restaurant and wearing his filthy boots. He squatted and took a bite out of his roll. He didn't get any peanuts because he couldn't grasp the small morsels with his bandaged hands.

A boy, no more than thirteen or fourteen padded up near Ward and likewise squatted. The youth was quietly crying and eating at the same time.

Ward held his roll out to the boy. "I don't need this. You are still growing."

A blow from a thick cane to Ward's shoulder turned his vision white. Several more blows left him writhing on the dirt. Without thinking, Ward cried out to his ancestors, and the intensity of the blows increased.

"Who is your god?" yelled Sixty-Four above the volume of the loudspeaker. "Tell me who!"

Sixty-Four and another guard dragged Ward across the dirt floor of the tent. By the time Ward's vision cleared, he was prostrate before the image of the Chairman. *Surely the guards don't think the Chairman is a god.* The thought made Ward convulse with laughter.

The other guard kicked Ward in the hip. "What's so damn funny?"

"I'm *here*, in my body," Ward said between his gasps of pain and his guffaws.

"What are you talking about?"

"Never mind that," Sixty-Four said as he stepped in with a quick strike of his cane. "Who's your god?"

Ward responded with a groan.

"Modern" *whack* "Colonists" *whack* "enjoy" *whack* (the last blow landed askance of Ward's shoulder and caught him in the head; he grew faint) "freedom" *whack* "from superstition" *whack*.

The beating stopped, and Sixty-Four yanked Ward to his knees. *On my knees, just like Patro.* A ripple of panic fluttered in his mind, but Ward brushed it aside.

The atrocious voice on the loudspeaker made Ward's eardrums prick with pain. *Every citizen is equal. There are no castes.*

Ward let out a little giggle. *Whack.*

Other prisoners seemed oblivious to the violence except for the boy. He dropped his food—and Ward's—and crabbed walked backward and disappeared under the table of peanuts.

From his kneeling position, Ward grinned up at the furious guard. "Hey, Sixty-Four, so long as I am no longer a killer, I am free. Don't you get it?" Ward broke out in a new wave of laughter until Sixty-Four snatched a sweet roll and shoved it in Ward's mouth, silencing him.

* * *

Later that day, the tired bus broke down on the way back to the prison. With twelve kilometers to go, the prisoners debussed while the driver and two guards made much ado about it over the radio.

"I'm very thirsty," said the boy. He sniffed, and his lower lip trembled.

"Try not to cry," the doctor said. "It depletes your body of fluids." He ran his long fingers across the top of his self-balding head until he came upon a wad of sparse hair. He yanked it out then lay on the side of the road with other reclining men who, in their various states of health and injury, appeared more like heaps of dusty tree limbs than men.

"Maybe when the other bus unloads it'll come back to get us," said one of the resting men.

Ward nodded. "It'd be the most logical solution until they fix our bus."

Soon, a truck arrived, and the sluggish men sat up. Ward's heartbeat quickened. They'd be going back to the camp soon. Food, water, toilets.

Guards emerged from the truck and unloaded three mopeds. The bus driver, Fifty-One, and Sixty-Four mounted the mopeds while the truck drove away empty.

"On your feet," yelled Sixty-Four. "We—" he indicated the bus driver and the other guard—"will escort you as you walk to the camp."

Moans and sighs filled the air as well as the boy's sobs.

What in the world could such a young boy have done to land him alongside adults who illegally quit jobs or who are violent or homosexual or street beggars? Ward glanced at the old doctor. *Or who are crazy?*

Ward shook his head and started walking, leading the other prisoners behind the slow motoring Fifty-One.

Both of Ward's yellow shoes cracked after eight kilometers and refused to stay on his feet. He left them on the side of the road.

* * *

That evening, the tenets played on a loop over the speakers as men squatted in the cafeteria and drank rice gruel from wide bowls and weak tea from plastic cups. The warm meal was unseasoned, but as Ward palmed the bowl with his bandaged hands and swallowed, the tasteless warmth washed the gravel dust from Ward's mouth and throat, and he was grateful.

Back in his cell, Ward lay on his cot and looked up at the tiny square window. His ears rang from the noise of the day, and he knew his hearing would suffer, but for now, the ringing was like a lullaby, and he fell into a peaceful sleep with the knowledge he hadn't been a killer that day.

* * *

Fay cancelled all the evening's dinner reservations as soon as Ward ran off. When he didn't show up the following day, she took over his job, but try as she might, her pitiful strikes only resulted in an impatient chef, late dinners, and thrashing dogs that, if they were heavy enough, strangled themselves before she had a chance to kill the simple-minded animals with the pole.

"A restricted airflow is okay, good in fact," the frustrated chef said, "but don't let them die from asphyxiation."

"Why does it matter?" she asked him. She was desperate to get food on the table for her customers. "Why can't they simply choke to death?"

"The lower pH from the restricted air plus the hormonal changes from the pain you inflict makes the meat tastier." The university-trained chef went on to describe the specific blood chemical markers in scientific terms.

His explanation went over Fay's head, but she nodded as he spoke because she trusted the man and his culinary talents. He taught her to avoid striking the head or spine. If she knocked a dog unconscious or broke its spine, it wouldn't feel enough pain before death.

She resolved to improve her slaughtering skills.

Once, when she missed on a swing and lost her balance, she stumbled into the vicinity of the dog's teeth and received a nasty bite on her arm. She had the cadre wrap her arm in cheesecloth from the kitchen and went back to work on the dogs.

After Ward had been gone a fortnight, Fay's hands were covered in weeping blisters. In desperation, she tried switching to a hammer. The heavier tool was more effective with her small stature, but the chef complained of broken bones. *It's not possible to dress the meat properly with all these broken bones,* he had said. She didn't understand why not, but once more she trusted the chef and started using the pole again.

As Fay's blisters began to callus over, she developed tendonitis in both elbows.

"You should close," said the cadre as she palmed some of the chef's grated ginger and aggressively rubbed it on Fay's elbows.

Fay winced. The cadre may as well have been using the grater itself.

"Close the restaurant for a while, a few weeks at the most," the cadre said.

"Never!" *I'd lose customers. I'd lose money.*

When yet another week passed and Ward hadn't returned, the restaurant cadre told Fay that Ward wouldn't be back for a longer period of time than expected. "It could be months," the cadre said.

* * *

It took two weeks for new skin to emerge from beneath the scabs on Ward's hands. He and the doctor spoke of politics and philosophy on the bus when the guards were out of earshot, and in the night, too, after the loudspeaker had gone silent and their low voices echoed off the hard walls and traveled easily from cell to cell. Sometimes Ward thought he had misjudged the doctor, that the doctor was sane and simply determined to take a stand any way he could.

Or worse, maybe the old man is perfectly sane, and I've gone mad. "I am happy," said Ward, continuing his thoughts out loud. "I'm in prison, and I'm happy."

"Me, too," replied the doctor.

"How? You can't practice medicine."

The doctor laughed. "I healed your hands, didn't I?"

Ward nodded even though his new friend couldn't see him.

"Why are you happy?" asked the doctor. The old man's words came out slurred. He sounded sleepy.

"In here I am not a killer."

The doctor's yawn seeped through the air. "Interesting."

"Do you think I've gone mad?"

"No, not at all. The mind is a powerful thing. Obsessions, nervoj, dissociation—dissociation, now there's a powerful one. Dissociation is like chopping a goldfish in two. The tail that flop-flops on the butcher block is independent of the mouth that gulp-gulps at the air. Separate, but of the same fish." He yawned again before continuing. "Delusions, addictions, paranoia. They're all just the brain's way of protecting the self."

Soon the old man's rhythmic breathing joined other nighttime sounds of the prison. A man's muffled sobs, a guard's footsteps.

Ward's weary muscles sagged into his thin mattress.

Someone singing.

Ward closed his eyes.

His eyes snapped wide open. "That's jazz, an American jazz song!" Ward propped himself up on his elbows. He hadn't heard jazz music since he was a child, before it was banned. His father's fingers would stab the keys, and Ward would watch and wonder how such beautiful music could come from such violent strikes at the ivory.

Sometimes his mother would sing along. Panjo's voice wasn't strong, not at all like the talented street musicians and stage performers, but lovely nonetheless—clear and precise, like the song thrush.

He lay back down, lacing his fingers behind his head, and fell asleep and dreamed of his mother's melodic voice.

* * *

His mother's arms squeezed his little-boy chest as the two of them huddled in the corner. A soldier yanked on her arm.

Panjo screamed and pleaded with the wild-eyed soldier. "My son has no one else. If you take me, too, there will be no one to care for him."

"That's not our problem," replied another soldier, the one poised by the piano with a sledgehammer.

The soldiers were angry, so angry. The family's front door stood ajar, and the soldiers tramped about the living room, knocking books off the shelves and smashing icons with sledgehammers and cane sticks. Ward pushed against Panjo's chest, trying to force his way inside his mother's torso to get away from the angry men.

Patro crawled on his knees first to one soldier then the next. "We have done nothing wrong," he said. Patro's protests brought a swift cane to the back of his head.

"Patro!" Ward yelled, and his mother pressed his mouth shut with her quivering hand.

Ward's father bled and wept while the soldiers burned books and the bookshelves that once held them. Smoke turned the ceiling black and made it hard to breathe. Then the angry men attacked the piano with their sledgehammers, and the discordant wails from the dying instrument joined the cries of Ward's parents.

* * *

Ward woke in the prison hallway, his bare heels dragging on the concrete.

What's going on?

Two guards he had never seen before were dragging him toward the exit. When Ward tried to twist out of their arms, the bigger of the two guards jabbed Ward in the ribs with a rifle butt.

"Where are you taking me?" Ward peddled backward to rise to his feet only to stumble again. He couldn't walk backward as fast as they were dragging him.

Outside, the stars were throwing a party, and Ward thought it ironic how beautiful the sparkling sky was in such an ugly place as a prison. Out here he could see actual stars instead of his usual view of city lights reflecting off smog. And yet, out here with these two men, he knew something that was anything but beautiful was about to happen.

The wails of imprisoned wives and mothers carried through the night air from the far side of the camp, and Ward silently asked the ancestors to give the women and his own mother good dreams.

The three men arrived at a small outbuilding, and Ward was finally able to stand while one of the soldiers opened the door. It was a cinderblock shack with a bare bulb, a table and chair, a pen, and a stack of paper.

Ward read the patch of the guard who had hit him with a rifle butt. "Thirty, I've never seen you before," Ward said.

He read the other guard's uniform patch. "And One-Forty-Five, who are you?" The second guard carried only a cane stick, no rifle.

No rifle? That's different. "I've been here approximately four weeks," Ward said. Four weeks was just a guess because all the days were the same and blurred together. On second thought, maybe it was more like four months. "After all this time, I've never seen either of you. What's going on?"

"Sit," said Thirty.

Ward sat. "What's going on?" he asked again.

One-Forty-Five stepped forward. "Write your apology to our Chairman for abandoning your duty to the Modern Colony."

"Every job is important," said Thirty, citing the tenet.

The two guards left Ward in the shack, slamming the metal door behind them. Ward pushed the pen and paper away, and it reminded him of another time he had pushed pen and paper away.

He was young back then, perhaps eight, and his mother was helping him with his logograms. Ward's childlike ink marks bounced around the page like discarded tree branches. He wanted neat logograms in neat rows like his mother's. He had pushed his paper away in frustration.

Panjo, I miss you. Ward laid his head on the table. He was exhausted from gravel work, but he couldn't fall asleep in the shack. It was too quiet and too small.

In about half an hour, as far as Ward could estimate, the guards returned.

"You've written nothing," said Thirty. The big guard shoved Ward's chair against the table and leaned on it, pinning Ward's chest. It was hard for Ward to get a full breath.

"Write an apology?" Ward scoffed and then wished he hadn't wasted his precious breath. "I will not apologize for abandoning my job."

One-Forty-Five slapped the table. "What are you talking about? Every job is important."

"No, it is not important," Ward said with a wheeze, "to torture a dog to death."

Thirty let go of the chair. "It is *my* job to ensure you contribute to the Modern Colony." He swung his rifle like a club, beating Ward across the back and shoulders. Ward shook with pain. With another blow, this one to the side of Ward's head, his vision turned black, and he dropped into unconsciousness.

* * *

The morning loudspeaker blaring the same tired tenets woke Ward up. At least in the city he had gotten news along with the tenets.

How is Li Ling? What is she doing this very moment?

Ward looked left and right. He was back in his cell, but on the floor instead of his cot. He stood up, surprised at the strength of the pounding pulse in his head and how difficult it was to lift his arms.

The bumpy bus ride and the banging hammers were especially painful to his tender head that day. At the gravel mine, for the first time, he worked slowly.

There was a disturbance behind him, and Ward turned to see a guard he didn't know with a brutally mangled arm. Guards and prisoners alike were calling for the doctor.

"Dok, venu!"

"Dok, hurry!"

"Get the Dok!"

Prisoners everywhere stopped working and looked in the direction of the commotion. Ward's aged friend ran two feeble-legged steps toward the pleas for help then stopped.

"No," the old man said, and men nearby cussed and cast sidelong glances at each other. The doctor spat. "I will not help a Colony lackey."

Sixty-Four was upon the doctor before the doctor finished his sentence. The first swing of the angry guard's cane brought a cracking sound that caused nearby prisoners to cover their mouths in horror.

Ward lunged at the guard. "Stop, he's old. You'll kill him!"

The guard caught Ward in the neck with the end of the cane and forced him off balance. Ward hit the ground with his neck bent forward, and a strange, new pain like the fire of a toothache exploded from his neck through his bruised shoulders.

Ward blinked at the dusty sky, unused to feeling such agony. His stomach retched at the thought of what the dogs had gone through, all the dogs he had killed.

And the doctor, how the doctor is suffering now!

Ward rolled over and let out a cry of pain. He rose to his feet and ran to help his friend. The ground swayed with each of his footsteps, and his vision faded in and out.

"Dok!" Ward screamed. *I'm coming, doctor! Hang on, friend, I'm coming!*

"Get up!" yelled Sixty-Four as he struck the fallen doctor again and again. "Get up, you stupid, old fool, and help our comrade!"

The doctor's limp body failed to respond. Ward stumbled to a stop.

The red, fleshy soup around the doctor's head told Ward his friend would never get up again.

* * *

The next days passed in a blur. Bus, tenets, the shack, beatings, his cell, gruel, gravel, bus, tenets. It could have been six days or six months, Ward didn't know. The midnight trips to the shack were scrambling his brain from lack of sleep as well as from repeated head trauma. Often he could hear the prisoner boy crying—or was it Ward himself sobbing?—and sometimes the boy's crying was like the drone of human-sized hornets or the hiss of books aflame.

"Your mother," One-Forty-Five said. They were in the shack, and One-Forty-Five stood over Ward while he sat at the table.

In his stupor, Ward didn't remember picking up the pen. He had written the Chairman's name. When had he done that? Were those his logograms?

Ward rubbed his eyes. "Panjo?"

"What has she done to insult the Modern Colony?" One-Forty-Five said.

Ward stood up so fast that he knocked the chair over. With a movement too swift for Ward's tired eyes to see, Thirty countered by slamming his rifle into the back of Ward's legs. His knees buckled and hit the floor, and his nose struck the table with such force it made his eyes tear up. He sniffed and tasted blood in his throat as he knelt before the ancestral shrine—

No, not a shrine, a table. The shack. My re-education. There was blood on the table. *When did that happen?*

Thirty smirked. "She likes her job, doesn't she? A smart woman with a smart job."

The floor was cold against Ward's knees. He missed the doctor. Ward wondered how long had it been since he'd seen his old friend. He recalled the most recent mass shower—an outdoor spray-down of stripped prisoners—being icy cold. The doctor hadn't been there.

It wasn't so cold now. It wasn't hot, either. He remembered what hot was. Hot was when sun-baked rocks blistered the soles of his feet until he had learned to dig shallow footholds before squatting with his hammer and chisel.

He ran his tongue around his mouth in an effort to get rid of the bloody taste and discovered that he'd lost a molar. His tongue probed the space. It was healed over, so it had been a while.

"I ask you again," One-Forty-Five said, "what has your mother done to insult the Modern Colony?"

Ward looked up at his captors. "How long does it take for a tooth to rot and fall out?"

The two guards exchanged puzzled looks.

"Your mother," One-Forty-Five said through clenched teeth.

A burn flooded Ward's eyes and nose, and then his face felt puffy. It had been so long since he cried, he had forgotten what it felt like.

"Nothing!" Ward yelled. He started trembling. "She has done nothing!"

Thirty crouched so he was eye-level with Ward. "Wrong," said the guard. "She made you." He stood and laughed at his own joke, and the other guard joined in.

"I will be happy to teach her the tenets," said One-Forty-Five.

"No, no!" Ward crawled toward the men. "She is good. She made a good son. I will do my job. I will do my job. *I will do my job!*"

TRI

(Three)

Without ceremony, the soldier-driver stopped the sedan in front of Ward's apartment building. Ward climbed out. It was spring of 1988, and he was home.

The daytime cadre was smoking on the front stoop. "You've been gone awhile," he said with a snicker as Ward approached. "Not a very smart one, are you?"

Ward went upstairs and stopped to use the restroom. He gasped when he saw his reflection in the mirror. His face and neck were so dark from working such long days in the sun that he looked like he was born and reared a peasant.

Someone had replaced the doorknob to Ward's apartment. Inside, a blanket of yellow-gray dust lay across the floor and furnishings, all except his desk chair which looked like someone had been sitting on it. He looked in his dresser. His only remaining pants and shirt, besides the camp uniform he was wearing, were still there. He changed into them.

He opened the desk drawer. His tin box was still there. The money was still inside.

The room smelled faintly of his mother.

His books were gone. Ward hoped it wasn't the soldiers who had taken them but residents, to sell or to learn English. He eyed his bed. Perhaps his favorite book was still hidden under the mattress.

Someone knocked on the door, and Ward's stomach leaped to his throat. Then he reminded himself he was home, safe.

"Come in," he said.

Lam smiled. "You're back." She rushed in, her arms wide as if to hug him, and at the last second, she grabbed his hand and shook it with both of hers. "I missed you. We missed you." She was still shaking his hand. "That night, I'm sorry, the soldiers woke me up. I—"

"No, you had to."

She dropped his hand and stepped back, looking him up and down. "Are you okay? Because you look different."

My dark skin. "Have you seen Panjo?" *And shoes, I have no shoes. I am a peasant.*

"Your mother? I see her every Saturday. She comes and sits and waits for you, and then she leaves after an hour. Are you sure you're okay? Come have lunch with me. I can tell you all about my son's classes." Lam smiled as she spoke, but she wrung her hands when she mentioned school.

"No thank you. I have errands to run."

Lam's smile faded. "Oh, okay. Well, I'll see you around."

* * *

After Lam left, he gathered three dolaroj, *dollars,* in coins from his tin box and walked barefoot down to the street vendors. He bought a pair of purple plastic shoes. From there he went to the Smits' tailor shop.

39

Their shop was on North Prosperity Street next to the city's biggest bicycle store. Each business brought traffic to the other.

The Smits' shop, narrow but long, stretched all the way to the alley in the rear. Side-by-side sewing machines lined the walls of the shop, and stacks of shirts and trousers, sorted by size, sat on tables near the cash register at the front. The younger, newer employees had to work outside on the front stoop, squatting before their machines. Almost everyone in the city wore a white shirt and loose-fitting, navy pants from the Smits' shop.

Ward bought a pair of pants, but they didn't have a shirt his size.

The clerk, the Smits' daughter, waved an arm at all the sewing machines and workers. "We can make you a shirt in forty-eight hours."

He declined, balking at the price.

Passing a neighborhood wet market on the way home, Ward spotted a coolie hat in a large garbage can and dug it out. The headband that held the hat elevated above the wearer's head to allow for airflow was broken, but Ward could easily mend it with a piece of duct tape. The broad brim would keep the sun off his face and neck.

The irony that he was going to use a peasant's hat to keep his face from looking like a tanned peasant's wasn't lost on him.

When Ward got home, he checked under his mattress and smiled. Alice and the Cheshire Cat stared at Ward from the cover of his favorite banned book.

He retrieved his jacket from the bottom drawer of his dresser, not because it was a chilly spring day, but because it had pockets. Slipping the literary contraband in an inside pocket, he headed back out.

Instead of stopping to eat lunch in the cafeteria, he simply pocketed a steamed roll and took a long walk down to Northwest Teacher's College. He waited in the shade of a ginkgo tree. Nearby, a group of students squatted in a circle and quizzed each other on physics problems.

Soon, Ward spotted and approached a young man passing between buildings with a stack of textbooks between his bulging biceps. The student's shoulders were just as broad and his chest just as thick as Ward's.

Half an hour later, in a dim dormitory stairwell lined with handmade protest posters—*Freedom of the Press! End Political Corruption! March on Capital City!*—Ward traded his book for an unstained, white shirt.

Ward pointed with his chin at the posters. "I've seen protests get out of hand," he said, meaning the chaos during the Civil Revolution. The student was too young to have remembered the Revolution. "Be careful."

The student shook his head. "I don't attend school to protest, only to study. Besides, I don't think their protests will amount to much." It turned out the young man was an urban transportation management student, and for a moment Ward pictured himself in the young man's stead. Advanced math, mechanics, city planning.

As Ward was leaving the dormitory, a craving grew in his throat, traveled downward, and settled somewhere behind his sternum. To quell the craving, he took out the roll he had nabbed from the cafeteria and started eating it. Sugared bean curd filled the roll, and his taste buds jumped to life. As he ate, he passed between the buildings where so much learning took place.

He finished the roll and looked back at the college's buildings. As delicious as the treat had been, his craving remained.

KVAR

(Four)

Fay squatted in the shady doorway at the back of her restaurant and eyed Ward as he worked in the late August heat. He had returned one day in spring after being gone eighteen months for re-education. Although he had picked up right where he had left off and hadn't missed a day since, she still hated him for leaving her in a bind.

She had opened the restaurant a decade ago, choosing its name and menu from the popular summer festival in China. With no competitors in the city and a proficient chef, business was good.

Until Ward's flight.

Fay clenched her teeth. She was aware that she was glaring at Ward, but she didn't care. Besides, Ward was working in the sun and wouldn't be able to see her in the dark doorway.

Just one dog today. A family was coming in from Victory City on the evening train.

Ward rarely spoke now, never smiled. He walked hunched over with his eyes cast down. Fay refused to feel sorry for him. *He deserves it. The troublemaker should have never left his job.*

He squatted, noose in one hand, the other hand held out to entice the dog he had selected, a terrier of some kind. Fay never bothered to learn the specific breeds. They all tasted the same according to her customers if they were prepared properly.

The terrier loped toward Ward and sniffed his hand as Ward deftly slipped the noose over its head.

He's certainly a lot better at it than I was. Fay massaged her forearm where the dog had bitten her. Her skin was scarred and lumpy now.

* * *

When Ward was gone, Fay never did get good at slaughtering the dogs, and her elbow tendonitis was the final straw. She had to figure out a way to kill the dogs while not injuring herself (or getting bit), and she couldn't use the hammer if she wanted to keep the chef happy. Most importantly, she had to kill the dogs efficiently so the customers wouldn't be kept waiting.

After a particularly painful night when Fay's aching elbows kept her from sleeping, she climbed out of bed early in the morning. She padded her wire bicycle basket with pages from her trade magazine—*The People's Restaurant*, "Air Conditioning Coming to Popular Capital City Diner" and "Efficient Goldfish Ponds for Seafood Restaurants"—so that her cargo on her long journey back wouldn't rattle about. She rode her bicycle forty kilometers north, past the technology region of the city, and past the fancy apartments of the Press workers.

The magazine pages flew out of the basket as Fay cycled. She stopped to chase down the pages the first few times as scowling pedestrians yelled at her for clogging the sidewalk with her abandoned bicycle, but as she grew tired, she cared less and less about the loose pages. Soon her basket was empty.

As the city thinned, she expected a soldier to stop her and ask for her travel permit, but none ever did. Perhaps the only people who wanted to go to and from the mountain villages north of the city were the peasants themselves.

Fay spat. *Peasants. Why are the dirtiest, most stupid people in the Modern Colony the wealthiest?* "The Colony is a land of contradictions," Fay said as she leaned into the wind and peddled harder.

She rode past a tree stump that had been carved into the image of a Great Hornet, the mountain people's god. *Even after the Revolution, the ignorant peasants cling to their superstitions.*

When the asphalt ended at a dirt crossroad, Fay turned right toward the village at the base of the Blue Mountains. She hadn't been to the village since the Civil Revolution when she worked the fields under the supervision of uneducated, uncultured, maddeningly superstitious peasants and slept with other workers in mud-brick barracks they built themselves.

The barracks were gone now, and the village smelled of weedy clover, sweet hay, and a mineral-rich wind that swept down from the rock-faced mountain ridge. Fay's shoulders relaxed. She didn't know what she expected, but this bucolic village was far different from the prison-like entity it had been during the revolution.

The first cinderblock house she encountered was modern and so big she thought it was a store, but then she realized it was a home. Peasant families could afford such extravagance. *Someday me, too, in Lockridge. When I open my restaurant there.*

Fay could picture it. A fancy, modern restaurant where wealthy tourists would dine. It would be a vegetarian restaurant. Outsiders liked vegetarian dishes, and Fay would set the menu prices high. There'd be bright, electrical lights overhead, a polished, wooden floor, and even music on a CD player. *Ha-ho! The chef thinks we can open a restaurant in Capital City, but he doesn't understand. Our northern accents would never be accepted there. "Peasants!" they would say.*

Fay spotted a boy about twelve or thirteen riding a water buffalo through a dusty, mung bean field. The boy was shirtless, his shoulders dark from the sun. She waved him down, and he slid off the beast and came toward her while the water buffalo moseyed over to a fallow area.

"Where can I find your parents?" she asked him.

"Inside, I'll show you." He took her hand with his. His fingernails were black with dirt, and Fay tried not to cringe.

Laughter greeted Fay as she and the boy entered the cinderblock house. Four women sat at a square table in the living room. They were playing Hearts with a fancy deck of cards, the kind with the intricately stamped images. Fay's deck had a solid-colored back. It didn't matter, though, because she had no one to play with anyway.

"Panjo," said the boy, "a visitor."

"Join us," the youngest of the women said and hurried to pull up another chair.

Fay shook her head. "Thank you, but I just wanted to buy—"

"Do you want to see my new pet?" asked the boy.

"I'm only here on business. Perhaps you can tell me where your father is," she said, but the boy had disappeared around the corner.

The boy's mother laid a card down in the discard pile. "He'll be back in a minute."

The boy or the husband? Fay didn't have time for this. Had peasants no sense of urgency? "I don't specifically need to talk to your husband. I just wanted to buy—"

The boy returned with a brown-haired creature in his arms. It had spiked ears, and as he brought the animal closer, it growled.

Fay stepped back, and the women at the table laughed.

"It's just a rabbit," one of the older ladies said. She got up and took Fay's hand and guided it over the rabbit's back.

Soft, as if my fingers were drifting through a cloud. She had seen

45

drawings of rabbits, of course, but never one in real life. Fay soon realized the animal wasn't growling. It was purring.

The boy's father came back from wherever he had been, and Fay was able to negotiate a price for a used bolt gun and a set of blank cartridges.

As she placed the bolt gun in her bicycle basket, the mother gave her a peach for her journey.

"Come back and visit," said one of the other ladies.

The boy gave Fay a Polaroid photo of himself, and Fay couldn't help but smile.

Then she got on her bicycle and headed back. It was a loud return trip with the bolt gun rattling in her bicycle's wire basket, but even with all that noise, she could hear the morning news on the loudspeakers as she approached the city.

After the news—"events that are of significance to citizens of our Modern Colony"—Li Ling recited the tenets. Today she also mixed in bits of healthful advice. "Only drink boiled water."

Fay arrived at her apartment with a sore bottom and an achy back.

"Everybody has a job. Every job is important," said Li Ling.

Fay was not used to such exercise, and she moved stiffly. Her daily bicycle commute from her apartment to the restaurant was only two city blocks.

"Sleep eight hours every night."

Fay never even pushed the restaurant cart down to the farmers market. The chef and his assistant did that.

"Every citizen is equal. There are no castes."

By the time Fay finished washing up, it was past noon, and she could barely walk. She put the bolt gun and cartridges in a bag and hobbled out the door of her apartment. After giving her bicycle some consideration, she thought it best to walk to work today. She bought two bowls of chicken-flavored rice and a glass of tea from street vendors on Citizens Street and then hobbled some more to the restaurant. Using the bolt gun, she went to work on that evening's dogs.

Customers complained. The meat didn't taste the same.

In the hot, humid kitchen, the chef folded his arms and huffed. "I can't serve dishes like this," he said, wrinkling his nose in disgust. "The quality isn't as good as when Ward was here."

"And I can't slaughter dogs the way he could." If her legs weren't so sore, she would have kicked the pompous man squarely in his kneecaps. "You'll have to slaughter the dogs yourself if you don't want me to do it. You can come in earlier, before you do the prep work with all the vegetables."

"No. No, no," the chef said. He pinched the bridge of his nose as if he were getting a headache. "Without refrigeration, the meat won't last long enough if we slaughter the animals before prep. If we slaughter the animals after prep, then the vegetables won't last. *You* have to slaughter the animals or apply to the government for someone to replace Ward."

Fay knew the chef was right. The very next morning, she dragged her still-sore body to the bus stop cater-corner her apartment building. She would apply for a replacement slaughterer right away. If the job was left to her and the bolt gun, the restaurant would lose money. She might even have to close.

And she'd come so far on this Modern Colony entrepreneurial journey!

I must not give up. Think positive, Fay. To distract herself, she studied the advertising posters surrounding the bus stop.

First was a poster with the tenet *Every citizen is equal. There are no castes.* An image of a peasant man in his work clothes and a city man in his business clothes, each with an arm around the other's shoulders, accompanied the tenet. The two figures were so close together that they shared the shade of the peasant's coolie hat.

Fay remembered the boy and his rabbit and couldn't help but smile.

Next was Colony Radio Morning's poster featuring Li Ling's face. Li Ling's poster was the biggest of all the ads. Her face was as captivating as her voice. The perfect symmetry of her features, her moon-shaped face (the epitome of feminine beauty in the Colony), and her curvaceous lips painted the color of success: poppy red.

Fay folded her arms. Beauty wasn't the only way to make it big in the Modern Colony. *I can too. It simply takes business smarts, menu items the customers want, and a skilled chef.*

The bus arrived, and she rode it uptown to the Regional Colony Office and picked up paperwork to apply for a new slaughterer. She submitted the paperwork to the restaurant cadre that afternoon.

The cadre shook her head and handed the paperwork back. "Ward will return."

Fay rolled her eyes then covered the rude gesture as if she were simply checking the cloud cover. "How do you know?"

"Did you give him a release letter?" The cadre's jaw tensed.

"No, I didn't *let* him go. He ran off!" She took a slow breath. Fay had spent hours on the paperwork, skipping both breakfast and lunch, but it would not be good if she upset her restaurant's cadre.

The cadre narrowed her eyes. "Then did you put him on probation as required?"

I have to put him on probation? "Never mind," Fay said.

She threw the paper away.

The restaurant lost business as Fay continued to use the bolt gun and wait for Ward to come back. She went home every night and dreamed of his return, of how she'd greet him with a few swings of the slaughtering pole upside his stupid head.

* * *

Ward glimpsed his boss squatting in the shadowed doorway. She'd been doing that a lot since he got back, especially this past week. He couldn't make out her face but felt her scowl, her hatred. It crept from the doorway across the courtyard and shimmed up his spine and came to rest on his shoulders, heavy. While he was gone, he hadn't realized the bind he'd put Fay in. He slumped under the weight of her hatred and his guilt.

Ward picked up the bamboo pole and faced the restaurant's still living Tuesday night dish.

Suddenly, from the shadow of the doorway, Fay charged him, teeth bared, growling.

"You set me back years, you weak, pitiful man," she screamed and slammed into him. The only effect the impact from her small body had was to make him take a short step back.

He looked down at his petite boss. If he used the bamboo pole on her, she would die faster than the dogs. She had such a pitiful layer of flesh over her vital organs. At least the dogs had some muscle, but what did Fay herself do? She stood around and barked orders at her staff or whimpered at her customers while her muscles shrank and her hands grew soft.

He, on the other hand, especially after his time at the gravel mine, had the strength of ten men in his hands. He could simply wrap his fingers around Fay's neck or, say, the handlebar of her bicycle and twist. Of course, that would be the act of a madman, and soldiers would come again in the dark hours of night and haul him off at gunpoint.

Ward did it anyway—vandalized her bicycle—after he finished his work that evening. He wasn't sure why he did it, but it made him feel better until his next dinner kill, and it was certainly better than wringing her actual neck. He was a killer, yes, but not a killer of human beings.

Fay walked to and from the restaurant now, and the weight on Ward's shoulders was heavier than ever.

* * *

The following Wednesday, Ward could feel Fay's eyes on him again as she paced behind the restaurant. She kept pausing to poke her head in the kitchen door and bark an order, and then she'd resume pacing, sometimes stopping to paw at the ground. She lit a cigarette and tossed it on the ground after only one inhale.

"Why are you watching me?" Ward asked. He opened a cage, and two black shepherd mixes leaped out. They had arrived together and were probably siblings. "Are you going to charge at me again?"

Fay stopped pacing. "No. Just don't mess up dinner." She scuffed the ground with her toes as if she would charge anyway, but maybe she was putting out her cigarette. She came closer.

"Can I use the bolt gun?" Ward asked for the third time that week. He braced himself in case she attacked him again.

"No, quit asking me that," she said.

"Can I use it on myself?"

Fay took a step back. "On yourself?"

"I'm suicidal."

She looked him over from his slouching shoulders to his feces-and-blood speckled boots. "I understand why," she said, her voice a smidgeon kinder. "Should I tell the cadre?"

Ward's heart thumped wildly as he remembered One-Forty-Five's threat. Ward pictured Panjo making gravel, writing letters in the middle of the night. *The wails from the women's wing.*

"No, Fay. I'll do my job." His heart raced. "I'll do my job."

Fay started toward the building, but she hesitated outside the door. "I need to serve perfect savory and spicy dishes tonight," she said, "for the Smits and their guests." Her voice cracked.

Ward looked at her. "Not the tailors."

"Yes, the tailors."

Ward understood Fay's nervousness, then. The Smits weren't luminaries, not like, for example, Li Ling, but the Smits had benefitted from the government's 1975 Four Modernizations economic campaign, and ever since then, their shop had flourished.

It could be a high-dollar night for Fay. Summer was winding down. School had started. There was a fresh energy in the city.

* * *

Ward finished working about nine o'clock that night and headed home. It had been a successful evening for Fay, her most prestigious customers ever, her biggest cash night ever. Ward kept imagining five- and ten-dolaro bills filling her cash register. But no matter how many times he blinked or shook his head, the bills were covered in canine blood.

Lam was standing on the apartment stoop, holding the door open, while her ten-year-old son sat on the front steps. City residents rarely sat on stairs or curbs or retaining walls. That was a peasant-like thing to do. The boy was so big around the middle that his shirt fabric strained at each button. He was so ugly that his arms angled out to the side whenever he stood because there was no room for them to hang straight. He was so thick in the face that his eyes almost disappeared under the excess flesh. Uglier than an American. So ugly that he could no longer squat on the stairs because his belly was in the way. He sat instead.

Lam let go of the door and wrung her hands. "Please, Son, be a sweetheart. It's late, and we need to go inside. Just a little bit of homework." She stepped down to face the boy.

He turned away and crossed his big arms over his chest.

"I'll help you with your math," she said, her voice small.

Lam's eyebrows drew up and together, a pleading look that emphasized the wrinkles on her brow. Whether it was the sulfur-laden, industrial dust of the city coating her hair, or just age, her locks refused to reflect the light coming from the fixture above the apartment entrance. Her skin was dull, too. It was as if Lam was slowly turning to dust. She was not at all like when Ward first met her.

* * *

He was young then, seventeen, and had only just received his job placement. It was a cloudy day in late spring, and he was moving from his mother's apartment in the northern part of the city to his furnished apartment in this building. All of his possessions fit in the wire basket of his bicycle. He parked his bicycle among the others in the bike rack near the front entrance. Every bicycle looked the same: one-speed, black, weighty, too small for tall people, and too big for most children.

Owners had personalized their bicycles to distinguish one from another. A red ribbon tied to the handlebar or stripes scratched into the crossbar. Here was one with snail shells glued to the back of the seat. Ward had borrowed a permanent marker and colored a musical note on the white trim of his bicycle's fender. Music, in honor of his pianist father.

Ward gathered his small bundle of clothes, the picture of his parents, and the precious English novels from his mother. He had hidden the novels within the clothes. They were books generally not allowed by the government, especially *Alice's Adventures in Wonderland* which was outright banned, but his mother worked with foreigners as a translator, and so allowances were made.

The apartment cadre met Ward on the stoop and told him his apartment number. Lam emerged in the hallway just as he reached his door. The small woman introduced herself. She smelled of chicken and garlic, and Ward's mouth watered. She spoke in a soft voice uncharacteristic to what citizens were taught to do in the Modern Colony, and she explained that she was married, but her husband worked and lived down in Victory City. "He has permission to travel every two weeks on the train, so we get to see each other twice a month." She giggled and color rose to her cheeks.

"Have either of you requested permission to transfer jobs so he wouldn't have to commute?" The books in Ward's arms were getting heavy, but he didn't mind. His gaze flashed to Lam's breasts before returning to her eyes.

She raised her voice, all business now. "We're applying for permission to get pregnant before applying for a transfer. There is a longer wait time for pregnancy, and since the cadre, no matter how kind he is, can only take one request at a time . . ."

Lam wore black leather sandals with silver buckles, a luxury. Ward was glad he was wearing his late father's equally fancy nubuck sandals.

Ward had never known anyone applying for permission to get pregnant, and the youthful, hormonal part of his brain imagined the act of conceiving.

"Hopefully you'll soon receive permission to get pregnant," he said politely.

* * *

A month after moving into his apartment, summer descended on the city. The city spent its nights regurgitating heat back into the air. Ward was returning from work amid the regurgitation when he encountered Lam on the sidewalk. She was with a slight man about ten years Ward's senior.

Sweat dripped off Ward's nose, and he was queasy. His stomach had not yet adjusted to the sounds and smells of his job.

Lam introduced the man as her husband, Holt.

A husband. Intercourse. He has intercourse with Lam. Even the thought of sex couldn't keep work-induced stomach acid from crawling up Ward's esophagus. He swallowed hard.

"We're celebrating," Holt said with a toothy grin that turned yellow under the sulfur glow of the nearby streetlight. "We're going for a stroll around the lake." His gaze slid over his wife's body then returned to Ward.

Couples often went to the manmade lake at The People's Park after sundown to hold hands or even kiss in the privacy of darkness away from city lights. With public displays of affection frowned upon, couples had to slip off to secretive spots. Ward still fantasized about visiting the lake with Li Ling.

With a flourish, Holt presented Ward a pack of Marlboro cigarettes.

American. "Thank you," Ward said, "but what is this for? And it's too much. I can't accept such a precious gift." He held the cigarettes out to Holt, who only smirked, then to Lam who responded by gently pushing Ward's hand away.

Lam giggled. "I'm pregnant!" She clapped her hands and proceeded to prattle on about children, school, family housing—"maybe we'll receive family housing before the baby comes. Imagine, an apartment with *two* bedrooms!"

Ward lived in a studio, so even Lam and Holt's current one-bedroom apartment sounded luxurious.

She turned toward her husband. "And Holt, we'll have to start attending parent lectures at the school. Did you know they changed the rule about parent lectures? Parents now have to attend starting the year *before* he enters kindergarten. And a name. We'll have to decide on his name."

"We hope it's a boy," Holt said in clarification. "We don't know yet." He pointed his effeminate chin at Ward. "What is your given name, Ward?"

Colonists typically called each other only by their surnames, unless they were celebrities. A married woman retained her surname, and children took on their father's name. Ward rarely had a reason to say his full name out loud.

"My given name is Kalb," he said. He snapped his mouth shut. He didn't like the taste of *Kalb* as it stumbled out of his mouth, but it was safe, a typical boy's name with the approved single syllable and four-letter maximum. It was a Middle Eastern name that meant *brave*.

In actuality, his real name was Benny. That was the name his parents had given him when he was born, before the Civil Revolution. Because of his father's musical inclinations, Ward was named after Benny Goodman, the American clarinet player.

In 1972 with the ratification of the Modern Colony statutes, Ward and all the other youth his age were forced to choose new names from the provided list. Similarly, Ward and his father had to drop the *Mc* prefix from *McWard*.

Lam's husband nodded. "Kalb Ward. Kalb is a noble name, one to consider." He thumbed his chest. "My given name is Brad, another fine name."

Brad meant *big*, and Ward bit his tongue so he wouldn't laugh at the small man with the big name.

The couple chatted on, but Ward's mind was on the cigarettes in his hand. *American, what a treasure!* The cellophane-wrapped package had crisp corners that poked Ward's fingers. He didn't smoke anymore, but the prized cigarettes tempted him. He brought the package to his nose. Any scent of tobacco was overwhelmed by the canine odors on his hand. He let his arm drop.

Lam was saying goodbye, and her husband had stepped away, apparently eager to get to the romantic lake.

Ward smiled and waved. "I'll ask the ancestors to bring you a boy," he said, hoping Lam and Holt wouldn't report him for superstitious beliefs.

That brought Holt back for a handshake. "Thank you, Kalb Ward. We appreciate that very much."

Instead of opening the cigarette package, Ward took the Marlboros inside the apartment building and rushed up the stairs two at a time, a fresh spring in his legs. He knew exactly what he'd do with the cigarettes first thing in the morning.

* * *

The sun streaming through the window tickled Ward's eyelids. He opened his eyes and grinned at the pack of American cigarettes on the pillow beside him. He sat up in bed and looked out the window. The normally smoggy sky appeared bluer this morning. He sniffed the cigarettes. Now that he was clean, he could smell their tobacco and mint flavors. Ward would ride his bike to the radio station and give Li Ling the pack of precious American cigarettes. He closed his eyes and envisioned her smile as she took them, felt her warm palm as she shook his hand in thanks.

Ward tucked the cigarettes in his breast pocket and bounded down the stairs and burst through the door into the sunshine.

His bike was missing.

Ward had lived at the apartment complex long enough to learn the distinguishing characteristics of the other bicycles. Perhaps someone had taken his by accident. There was the bicycle with the torn seat cover, one with the string wrapped around the crossbar, the red ribbon, the rusted bell . . . Ward's shoulders sagged as he came to the inevitable conclusion: Someone had stolen his bicycle.

He went back inside and down the first-floor hallway to the daytime cadre's apartment and knocked. A man in his mid-thirties with wet hair and smelling like soap answered the door. His chambray blue shirt hung unbuttoned.

"Someone stole my bicycle," Ward said.

Muscles in the cadre's neck tensed as he buttoned his shirt. "You don't lock it." Stepping into the hallway, he clipped his two-way radio on his belt. "When?"

"After nine o'clock last night and before just now."

The cadre relaxed and stepped back into his apartment. "Not my problem." He closed the door.

Ward raised his voice and spoke through the door. "What do I do?"

"Not my problem. Talk to the night cadre."

Ward fingered the cigarettes in his shirt pocket. *I'll take the bus.* He went back to his apartment and removed the tin box from his desk drawer. It was full of the extra fifty cendojn, *cents,* he had leftover from his paycheck every week after room and board. He didn't know what he was saving up for, but he'd keep adding coins to the tin until he knew.

Ward took two coins and left once again, this time to catch a bus.

He boarded the crowded red-line bus that went to the north end of the city. There were no seats available. It was a two-section bus with a pivoting joint, and he found a hanging grab-loop in the back section of the bus, behind the joint. At the next stop, more people crammed themselves aboard, and Ward cupped a hand over the cigarettes in his pocket to protect them. He was acutely aware that he and another man were now jammed buttocks-to-buttocks. With no room to maneuver, Ward tried to think of things other than his bottom.

Everything behind the pivoting joint was bouncier, and Ward couldn't tell if his stomach had that freefall feeling because of the bumps in the road that lifted him off his feet or because he was going to see Li Ling. Her presence had always made him feel that way.

At the next stop, a horde of men and women with black grease in their knuckles and on their pants got off. Mechanics. Ward shifted away from the man mashed against his buttocks. Women with freshly pressed Smit-brand shirts and men with newspapers got on.

At the following stop, a group of men wearing European business suits and carrying briefcases climbed on followed by a trio of shouting and laughing teenage boys. Ward stooped to read the street sign. He rarely came out here and didn't have the bus route memorized. A mother with her toddler was paused in the middle of the crossroad. The child squatted in his bright red, crotchless pants and defecated. Ward smiled to see such a cheery-colored clothing item and wondered if Lam's child would wear bright pants too.

There were fewer bicycles here and more cars, some private by the looks of them.

Ward heard the shouting youths' crude language and guffaws as they forced their way through the crush of passengers in the front half of the bus. The teenagers were no more than two or three years younger than Ward, but he felt a generation removed from such rude public behavior. As the trio neared, Ward stood straighter, puffing his chest out but keeping his hand over the pack of cigarettes. The youths pushed past on both sides of Ward. When the trio had safely passed, Ward pulled the pack out and examined it for damage. He grinned, still pristine.

The teenagers wore American shoes. One of them had Nikes. Ward was suddenly aware of how he stood out like a peasant with his stained shirt and tanned face. The tallest of the youths elbowed another, and they both snickered at Ward.

He got off several blocks early, not liking the way the three teenagers were looking at him. *I was stupid for taking the cigarettes out where they could see.* He was fine with walking a few extra blocks. Besides, his father's nubuck sandals were comfortable, and the leather straps were so soft it was like Patro's flexible, piano fingers were lovingly wrapped around Ward's feet.

The bus accelerated past Ward on the sidewalk, and his breath caught when he heard the guffaws and footfalls of the three teenagers behind him. They had debussed too.

He ran.

The slap of fashionable American soles followed.

As Ward approached the next intersection, he glanced over his shoulder only to turn back around and crash into a cluster of cyclists. He went down in a tangle of black fenders, spokes, and angry Colonists. The cyclists struggled to their feet and yelled at each other and at Ward.

"Watch it!"

"He's a thug!"

"Get off me!"

"Watch your baskets, he's probably a thief."

"Thief!"

As they righted themselves, Ward and the cyclists looked toward the oncoming youth.

A woman slamming her onions and tins of tea into her bicycle basket said, "He must have stolen from those children."

Ward tried to skirt the now upright cyclists, but two of the men grabbed him and shoved him into the oncoming youth.

The boys encircled Ward. He yelled for the cyclists to help, but they pedaled off in a collective harrumph. The trio tackled Ward, and he desperately clutched the cigarette package to his chest, unable to lash out at the youth with his fists while protecting the cigarettes. He kicked, but the biggest teen sat on his legs while the other two took off Ward's shoes.

The trio sprinted away.

Ward let go of his shirt pocket and the cigarettes. A sweaty fistful of cloth surrounded the crooked pack, its crisp corners gone. Shaking, Ward got to his feet. He straightened out the cigarette pack the best he could, but it leaned to the side like a life gone off course.

Ward walked barefoot the last couple of blocks to the radio station. The smell of his fear-sweat from the encounter with the youth grew strong. He kept checking door alcoves and the gap between parked cars for lurking teens, neglecting to watch where he placed his feet. He stepped in toddler feces on the sidewalk. It was warm and fresh and added to the stench already coming from his armpits.

Ahead, the radio station rose taller and sleeker than the older buildings surrounding it. Sharp corners cut into the sky. A twenty-something woman stood next to the door and picked at her fingernails. She could have been mistaken for someone waiting for a ride or waiting to meet up with a friend, especially since she had no two-way radio, but her crisp, chambray blue shirt told Ward she was a cadre.

Ward walked past, keeping his eyes down so as not to draw her attention. He crossed the street and pretended to stand in line at a street vendor selling bowls of pork-flavored rice. He had to let three other customers go ahead in order to keep from actually being first in line. The cadre pulled a cigarette out of her pants pocket and went around the corner of the building.

Seeing his chance, Ward dashed across the street and through the double glass doors of the radio station.

"I am here to see Li Ling," Ward told the receptionist.

"She's recording," said the bored-looking man. He was twirling a children's spinning toy between its two sticks, the blue and red plastic disk spinning faster and faster until it turned purple. A cup—a china cup, not a drinking glass that most citizens and street vendors used— of steaming tea sat atop a folded newspaper. The leaves at the bottom of the cup were still bleeding brown. It was a freshly made cup.

The receptionist put the toy down with a sigh and stood. "Why do you want to see Li Ling?" He crinkled his nose as if smelling something foul.

"She is my—" Ward closed his eyes and pictured Li Ling, her smooth hair, her moon face, her body that looked like Lam's.

Ward's eyes flew open. He shifted on his soiled, bare feet. *I haven't seen Li Ling in so long, it's no wonder I can't exactly picture her body.*

He glanced about while he tried to come up with an answer for the receptionist. The floor was tiled with red vinyl squares that gleamed with fresh wax. *She is my best friend from childhood. My dearest classmate. My first girlfriend, my pal, my confidant, the only girl I ever kissed.* The toddler feces drying on Ward's feet itched. He scratched one foot with the other, and some of the brown matter fell off. His face broke out in a sweat.

"Maljuna amiko," *Old friend,* Ward finally said.

"She knows you?" the receptionist asked, his eyes narrowing.

Ward nodded, and a bead of sweat threatened to drip in his eye. "I have a gift for her." He pulled the crooked cigarette pack from his pocket.

The receptionist eyed the cigarettes. "American," he said. His tongue slid across his lips as he held out his hand. "I'll give them to her."

Ward checked the double doors leading outside. The cadre hadn't returned yet. He could wait.

The receptionist's hand remained outstretched. "What name should I give Li Ling?"

Ward wiped the sweat at his eye with the back of his wrist and in doing so released a fresh waft of armpit sweat.

"Your name?" the receptionist said again and wiggled the fingers on his upturned hand.

Somewhere off to the side, an elevator chimed.

Ward's shoulders sagged. He slowly extended his arm and placed the cigarettes in the receptionist's hand.

"My maljuna amiko," Ward mumbled.

Ward left the building with his hands balled and thrust deep in his pockets.

He rode the bus as far as his remaining change would take him, then walked barefooted while mourning the loss of his father's gentle hands around his feet.

The next day Ward spotted a pair of yellow plastic shoes at a vendor's cart near the train station. He snatched them up. Their unique color made the pain of losing Patro's sandals more bearable.

* * *

Twelve weeks after he had taken the Marlboros to the radio station, Ward met a tearful Lam coming up the apartment stairwell. It was mid-afternoon on a Saturday, but only a little sun fought its way through the small windows above. There was one light bulb in the communal bathroom of each floor, and residents were allowed one per apartment, but there were no bulbs for the stairwell. Either daylight or streetlight kept residents from climbing stairs in pitch blackness.

A tear tumbled down Lam's cheek. She was slogging her way up the stairs as Ward was headed down.

"Kiel vi?" *How are you?* he asked her. Lam wore a purse that tugged on her shirt, exposing the feminine curve of her neck. Her skin was smooth but strangely pale, even in the low light, and he had an urge to wrap his arms around her soft body, protect it. He refrained.

"It was a girl. We aborted."

Ward understood their desire for a boy. Lam and Holt needed a boy so there'd be someone to take care of them in their old age. A girl was expected to grow up and take care of her in-laws, not her own parents. And yet, Panjo said reforms were coming, that everybody who worked in the city would have elder-age pension and group homes that would care for them.

"Perhaps—" He was going to say that perhaps by the time a baby girl became an adult things would be different, but Lam swayed, and Ward grabbed her elbows to steady her.

"I'm a little woozy," she said, "but I'm okay. I just need to rest. What were you going to say?"

Her breasts were still swollen from her terminated pregnancy, and Ward couldn't help but brush up against them as he steadied her. It was the first time he had touched a woman's breasts other than childhood hugs from his mother, and his breath quickened.

"Perhaps—" What *was* he going to say? Blood flow increased to his penis, and he tried to think of something else, anything else to squelch his lust. Muck boots, *Fahrenheit 451*, his missing bicycle, the slaughter frame at the restaurant. "Perhaps next time the ancestors will bring you a boy."

"My husband and I have already submitted forms requesting permission to try again." Her quivering lips curved into a weak smile, and she continued up the stairs.

* * *

Ward submitted his own paperwork—a request for a new job. He received an immediate response. Ward tore open the onion skin envelope and read the contents:

In accordance with the Colony Statutory Code 15.2, Section 1, requests for job transfers cannot be considered until applicant has been employed at current job for a period of no less than four years.

Application denied.

* * *

Over the next eight months, Lam had two more abortions.

But she finally did get pregnant with a boy. When that pregnancy grew into the third trimester, Ward's gaze often landed on her belly. It was so vulnerable, protruding like that. It was the first of her body to make its way past hungry diners in the cafeteria. It led Lam down the sidewalk and across busy streets. Her belly was the first of her body to board a bus or enter a dim stairwell. Only a thin layer of stretched skin protected the baby from the world.

Ward had nightmares.

In his nightmares, he'd be at work, just one dog that day, a female. She was noosed and hanging. The wind ruffled her black, silky fur. Her belly was exposed and vulnerable and swollen. In his recurring nightmare, he picked up his slaughtering pole and always started there, at the dog's swollen belly.

He'd wake up with his hands thrashing air and the sheets clinging to his damp body. He was positive the nightmares were messages from the ancestors. Lam's baby was in danger, and he urged her to be careful.

"Careful of what?" she asked. They were in the bathroom on a Sunday night after Holt had gone back to Victory City, and Ward was helping a very pregnant Lam wring the towels she just washed.

Ward glanced sidelong at her belly. *Careful of me. Of me, of me, of ME!*

She stared at his reflection in the mirror and then giggled. "You're a nervous one, aren't you?" She rubbed her palm in a circle over her belly. "I'm fine, Ward."

Despite Ward's foreboding dreams, no one ever did attack the fetus, and it lived, the boy, Lam's son.

* * *

As a baby, the boy wailed like every other child, but being the only baby in the apartment building, Lam and other residents rushed to his wailing side.

"I can take him for a walk in his baby carriage if you like, Lam," one of the men said as he nudged his way between Ward and the child.

Another time, when Ward and Lam were chatting at the communal bathroom sinks, a woman said, "Here, let me bathe him." The woman gleefully reached for the boy. "You go rest, Lam."

One Sunday when Lam and her visiting husband invited Ward for a glass of afternoon tea, she announced that she applied for and received permission to quit her job.

"No more daycare for our son," said Holt.

It was March of 1978, and the twelve-month-old child hadn't learned to crawl yet. He simply pointed to where he wanted to go, and Lam or Holt would rush to pick him up and take him across the room.

"What?" Ward blurted out. "How can you afford to live on one salary?" He clamped his mouth shut when he realized how rude he was being.

Lam chuckled. "It's a valid question."

Holt got up and moved his son from the middle of the living room to where the child was pointing, at the rattle on the floor below the window.

"We withdrew our request for a bigger, family apartment," Lam explained, "and Holt moved to a less expensive dormitory in Victory City."

Lam's son eventually learned to crawl, but only when Ward, who always watched the baby when Lam went to take care of chores for her widowed father-in-law, got down on the floor with the boy and repeatedly showed him how to crawl to the object he wanted, in this case, another educational toy that lit up and made various beeping noises.

Lam's son received many gifts. A bouncing ball from the old woman on the first floor, a warm nightgown from the couple across the hall.

The boy got used to the attention.

By the time he was three, his craving for onion-flavored rice had developed, but he fussed about the feel of the oil-slick onions, so Lam would get him a bowl of onion fried rice at the cafeteria and pick out the onion bits with her fork.

During one lunch when Ward sat with Lam and her son, the boy had grown impatient waiting for his onion-flavored rice. He soon turned red-faced and howled. Fellow diners urged Lam to "quiet that child," and Ward offered to take the boy outside.

Lam shook her head. "I'm hurrying," she said, her words clipped. She was feverishly picking through the rice.

When the woman sitting directly across from Lam got up and moved to another table, Lam pushed her fork aside and ran back to the breakfast line.

The boy wailed.

Diners scowled.

Out of breath, Lam returned with a pair of chopsticks, indisputably more efficient than a fork, and proceeded to deftly pluck the onions from the rice.

Ward couldn't watch anymore and got up and left.

He checked his mailbox as he'd been doing daily for the past two weeks. He'd been working at the Yulin Dish restaurant for four years now, so he had applied again for a job transfer.

An onion skin envelope waited in his mailbox. He grabbed it and ripped it open. He had five job offers all the way from the touristy city of Lockridge on the coast to the sprawling city of Shackleton known for its biotech research. Three of the offers came with studio housing. All five offers were dog slaughterer positions.

He threw the letter in the apartment incinerator.

*   *   *

"I'll take the boy to a street vendor and buy him a steamed roll," Ward said. It was a summer morning. He was in the cafeteria with Lam and her impatient three-year-old son, and she was busy plucking

67

onions.

"No," she said.

"You can eat your meal in peace."

She jabbed her chopsticks at him. "Why would I let you do that? My son is smart enough to know what he wants and ask for it. I am encouraging his intelligence." She turned from Ward with a huff and cooed at the boy. "You're going to be the smartest child in school."

A year later, when the boy was four, his appetite for onion-flavored rice had grown, and so had his body on the limited, high-starch diet. His young thighs were so ugly that they fought each other for space on the adult-sized cafeteria chair.

"In world news," Li Ling announced over the speakers as Ward entered the cafeteria for breakfast, "after a failed invasion, Argentinean forces have surrendered the Falklands to Britain. Colony Radio Morning, bringing you events that are of significance to citizens of our Modern Colony."

Ward chose pickled eggs then sat down next to Lam and the boy. Lam had not one but two bowls of onion fried rice on the table before her. With her chopsticks, she plucked the onions out of both bowls, tucking them into her mouth as she went, biting down exactly once before she popped the next minuscule morsel in her mouth. Her chopsticks moved so quickly Ward had a hard time keeping track of them. She ate with her elbow pointed at Ward like a weapon, as if guarding her son's rice against Ward's critical comments.

Her son crossed his arms and pouted. "Hurry, Panjo, you're taking too long!"

Lam's frantic eating reminded Ward of the way the dogs wolfed down restaurant scraps.

Some days when Ward ate with Lam and the boy, she spent money to get an extra dish for herself—residents were only allowed one free dish that came with the rent—and ate pork bits or sweet-n-sour fish, but she always had onions, too, because the boy always ate onion-flavored rice with the onions removed.

But one chilly winter day, Ward was warming up with a lunchtime bowl of the cafeteria's chicken-cabbage soup when Lam and her son joined him. The boy would be starting kindergarten in less than a year, but he was already as tall and as broad-shouldered as a second-grader. Around the middle, he was bigger than a pregnant mastiff. Shivering, Lam placed a bowl of soup and a spoon on the table for herself and another bowl and spoon on the table for her son.

Perhaps she was trying to assert herself, Ward thought, instill some discipline. More likely, she was just cold and trying to keep the two of them warm.

The boy banged his soup spoon on the table. "Panjo, that's not my rice. I'm hungry!"

Ward said, "Then eat your—"

Lam cut Ward off. "I'll take care of it." Her words were icy and sharp, but the circles below her eyes were lank and bruised with inadequate sleep.

Under the heavy glares of the other adults in the cafeteria, Lam begged her son in a hushed voice to calm down. She then went back in line and purchased a double helping of onion fried rice. When she returned to the table, the boy snatched the bowls of rice and shoveled the white grains into his mouth with his soup spoon, not even waiting for her to pluck out the onions.

Lam's expression softened. "Look at my big boy eating all those onions."

"He could have eaten onions all this time," Ward said, his temper rising. "Next time, leave him in the apartment with me while you eat." His own soup, now in his stomach, had been warm and savory and reminded him of his mother's soup. He pointed to her bowl which was certainly cold by now. "You could eat whatever you feel like, and when he got hungry enough, he would eat whatever you tell him to eat."

Her nostrils flared. "How dare you suggest I starve our—" Her cheeks reddened, and she lowered her voice. "I mean, how can you suggest I starve my child? He needs nutrition for his growing brain."

The dogs' restaurant scraps have more variety and nutrition.

* * *

On a Tuesday night the summer before Lam's son started kindergarten, Ward came home from the restaurant, and he heard the boy throwing a tantrum.

Ward knocked on Lam's door. She yanked it open.

"What?" She pressed her lips into a hard, flat line. Her eyelids were heavy, puffy. The canine death stench wafting off his body mingled with her onion smell. She had gone back to picking the onions out of the boy's rice.

"I could sit with him for a while," he said. "You could go out for a relaxing stroll."

Lam's stern face melted. "I'm sorry. I don't know why he makes such noise."

The boy had been watching the two adults interact. He balled his pudgy fists and squeezed his eyes shut so tight that his eyelashes disappeared. "Popcorn!" he yelled.

Ward turned his back on the child and pivoted Lam, too. "Is that what this is all about, popcorn?"

The boy screamed, and Lam twisted and reached for the child, but Ward held her in place.

Lam tried to shake free. "I know," she said. "I should have taken him to the street vendor's cart right after he heard the pop." She was referring to the explosion that happened when the pressure built up in the popcorn cooker. When the pressure-sensitive top blew open with a small *boom*, the popcorn was ready to eat.

Ward gasped. "What? No, it's too late for children to be visiting street vendors." He realized he was still gripping Lam's arm and released her for fear of hurting the woman.

"You're doing it again." She jabbed him in the chest with her delicate finger. "Our child—Holt and my child—will never be able to learn in school if he's upset all the time."

"Do you mean you're simply going to placate him?" When Ward was the boy's age if he had thrown a temper tantrum, his normally composed mother would have spanked him until her strength was drained. Corporal punishment of children was still legal in this part of the Colony. Ward itched to take a cane to the child.

"A happy child is a learned child," Lam said, quoting the tenet.

Ward threw his arms up. "The tenet is not about popcorn."

He turned and looked down at the boy's flushed face, and the child, perhaps understanding that he had an audience, stretched his mouth open for a fresh torrent of screams.

Lam tucked a plastic coin purse in her pants pocket and glared at Ward. "My son and I are leaving now." She held her hand out for the boy.

But Ward stepped between them. "No, a child his age shouldn't be out so late," he said, his volume rising to a shout by the end of his sentence.

Lam's mouth dropped open, and she stepped back.

He hadn't meant to scare her. He took a calming breath and said, "If you must feed him, you go. I'll stay."

Lam grunted her assent then smothered her son in kisses as he pounded his tubby fists against her thighs. "I'll be right back, my sweet. Ward will stay with you." She rushed out the door, her leather sandals slapping at her slender, feminine heels as she hurried away.

The boy struggled to get his own leather sandals on, presumably to go after his mother, but his young hands couldn't work the tiny buckles. Ward ignored the child and let him cry out his frustration.

When Lam returned with a cellophane bag of popcorn in hand, her son was asleep in the bedroom. He had exhausted himself with his emotional display, and Ward had carried the hefty boy into the dim bedroom—Lam always left the apartment's light bulb screwed into the living room socket—and pulled the cartoon character blanket over the sleeping child.

Lam looked from the bag to the closed bedroom door. "But what do I do with the popcorn?"

Ward grinned. "A bedtime snack?" He led the woman to the sofa. It was the hefty type that converted into a bed, and they sat side by side on the firm cushions. The upholstery smelled of onions and morning breath. Lam yawned as the two of them ate. After the popcorn was gone, Ward started to unfold the sofa for her, but he didn't want to send the wrong message. He fluffed the throw pillow instead. She lay down, and he took the afghan off the back of the sofa. By the time he pulled the crocheted blanket up to her chin, she was asleep.

KVIN

(Five)

"Son, I'll help you with your homework. We can do it together," Lam said, her words snapping Ward back to the present, to an August evening in 1988 following the Smits' dinner. Gone was the chubby five-year-old child who whined about popcorn. Sitting on the front steps under the glow of the entrance light was a huge ten-year-old adolescent who recently started his final year of elementary school.

The boy had grown a lot in girth while Ward was at re-education camp, and then some more in height over the past three months. Ward estimated the boy was sixty-five kilograms or about 140 pounds.

Lam wrung her hands while the boy ground the heel of his leather shoe into the concrete apartment steps. He chipped off a piece of aging concrete and scraped it across a stair. His shoes were not the school uniform clodhoppers most of his classmates continued to wear after school let out but a different shoe with perforated toes and waxed laces.

The daytime apartment cadre exited the building. The normally grumpy man wore a grin on his face and a white, civilian shirt on his back.

"Lam, did you hear?" the cadre asked as he slapped her on the shoulder. "It was all over the news today."

Lam angled her body away from the cadre. "No, I didn't hear," she said, her voice tense.

The cadre didn't seem to notice Lam's reluctance to engage. "We won in Seoul," he said, lifting a fist in celebration. "The Colony won *five* gold medals at the Olympics!"

He stepped toward the stairs but stopped at the sight of the sitting boy. The cadre raised an eyebrow at Lam. Lam's gaze dropped, and she shifted back and forth from one leg to the other in her plastic shoes.

Ward remembered Lam's leather sandals and the way they made a *pat-pat* sound as she walked. She sold them when her son was nine, and she got her cheap plastic shoes so the boy could have a set of comic books. He traded the books for an American candy bar that melted on his way home from school. He had eaten it anyway, or rather he slurped it while he sat on the stoop with the gooey chocolate mess all over the wrapper and his fingers.

Ward scrunched his upper lip as he regarded the ugly mound of flesh stationed on the stairs. Ward had obviously brought bad luck to Lam by giving away the American cigarettes during her first pregnancy. Maybe that first child was meant to be a boy and a studious, happy child. And now Lam was stuck with—Ward looked at the boy and sighed—whatever *that* was.

The apartment cadre harrumphed and bent down to the boy's level. The cadre whispered something Ward couldn't catch, and the boy's face paled. He hauled himself up, saying something about homework, and scrambled inside.

The boy's reluctance to study puzzled Ward. He had fond memories of school and of his parents' obvious pride as they corrected his homework. He'd heard that schoolteachers in America correct homework, not the parents, but that couldn't be true. How could one teacher, after working all day in the classroom, correct dozens of children's papers in the evening?

Maybe if the boy had a girlfriend he'd look forward to school. Li Ling had certainly made Ward's early years delightful, until the cursed placement exam.

* * *

Years ago, young Ward and Li Ling squatted side by side on top of the concrete retaining wall that separated their elementary school's lawn from the city sidewalk. Ward professed his love and said he'd do anything for Li Ling.

She smiled, and sunlight bounced off her cheeks.

"Anything?" she asked. Her gaze circled his face, fell to his hands, and explored them while his ears grew hot. She then returned her attention to his face.

Ward nodded vigorously. "Well, I wouldn't *kill* for you."

"Of course not, you silly boy." She leaned close enough that her breath caressed his neck. "Promise me that when we go to different classes next year you'll still be my best friend."

"I promise," Ward said. He spat. "Stupid placement exam."

"Stupid placement exam." She spat in agreement.

When Ward and Li Ling entered middle school the following semester, they set off on divergent educational tracks. Li Ling would be developing her literary and verbal skills while Ward was channeled into basic math and motor skills. He clutched desperately at their fading relationship, determined to keep his promise, but other than hellos in passing which happened less and less frequently, they never spent much time together, not like they had in elementary school.

* * *

The front door to the apartment building swung shut behind the boy, and Lam scrambled inside after her son. Slapping Ward on the back, the grinning, off-duty cadre wished him a good evening before strolling down the sidewalk.

Ward smiled in reminiscence of his childhood friendship with Li Ling, and he was confident her memories were just as fond. He'd still do anything for her, almost anything.

The boy didn't find a girlfriend that semester, or the next. "There are too many boys," he complained when Ward asked him about his classmates. "All the girls already have boyfriends." It was the spring of 1989, and the boy would soon take *his* placement exam.

* * *

Fay stepped out of her apartment and glanced at the brownish-yellow sky. Spring of 1989 was proving the smoggiest on record, but Fay smiled. The air was a comfortable, short-sleeve temperature, and the recent winter had been her restaurant's most lucrative season yet.

She'd already mailed her application and received permission to open a vegetarian restaurant in Lockridge with a choice of two currently empty locations she could rent. One was in a 1930s era building with European styling and a patio. The other was in a modern skyscraper with a view of the bay. Fay chose the older spot. She had read in her trade magazine that tourists liked patio dining. And it was all about the customer. She would take Ward, of course, rescue him from this life.

She rubbed her palms where blisters used to bloom and weep.

Fay would take the chef, too. He was arrogant and grouchy but good. Her dream was so close she could taste it. Just one more month at Yulin Dish, two months maximum. As long as nothing went wrong between now and when she received permission to move her personal residence. Then she'd let Ward and the chef know the good news so they could apply to move. It was all working out. She would have skipped down the sidewalk like a child if it weren't for the many people she would have crashed into.

The cadre was already at the restaurant.

"Kiel vi fartas, Fay?" *How are you, Fay?* the cadre asked in formal diction.

"I am fine, thank you," Fay replied in kind. Tightness grew in her stomach. Why was the cadre speaking with such formality?

"A Politburo representative will be touring the restaurant Friday."

"Tomorrow?" Fay gulped. Her recent tasks at the restaurant raced through her mind. Had Ward complained that she wouldn't let him use the bolt gun? *I should have been more compassionate when he said he was suicidal.* Had she insulted the cadre? Had one of her staff acted out?

A police vehicle with its siren on sped by out front, and the dogs howled, urging one another in choruses.

"It's part of the Four Modernizations evaluation," the cadre said when the dogs finally calmed down.

The Smits weren't the only people in the area who had benefitted from the Four Modernizations. Fay had opened her restaurant—naming it after the popular festival—with funds from the government's initiative. Fay and all eight of her staff officially worked for the city, but in unspoken truth, like the Smits' business, Yulin Dish was a private company.

* * *

Friday morning, Ward woke to the sounds of bicycle bells and car horns as the city began to stir. He had slept with the window open because of the pleasant spring temperature.

He grimaced. *How many will I kill today?*

Shaking off thoughts of work, Ward dressed and went down to the cafeteria for breakfast. He had an itch to read the newspaper, so after breakfast, he strolled past the garbage cans stationed between the food vendors' carts on Citizens Street until he spotted a newspaper among the trash. Other than a greasy corner, which he tore off, the paper was in good shape. He split it with an old man sitting cross-legged on a folding chair and selling handheld, bamboo fans. The fans snapped open with a flick of the wrist and folded to fit neatly in a pants pocket. Ward admired the craftsmanship but declined to buy a fan.

Newspaper tucked under his arm, he moseyed back to his apartment and spread the paper on his desk. He collected the thermoses full of freshly boiled water from outside his door and made a glass of hot tea. He yawned and stretched then settled down to read.

A familiar voice drew Ward to the window. *Panjo!* His mother usually visited on Saturdays, if she could get away, never Fridays.

Ward hurried and changed his blood-stained shirt for the clean one he had gotten from the college student. He hid his filthy muck boots under the bed but didn't have time to hide his coolie hat.

She knocked. The last thing Ward did before he opened the door was smile. He always tried to be happy around her because he knew she still felt guilty that she and Patro hadn't been able to talk authorities into letting Ward retake the placement exam. Ward's parents couldn't bribe his way into a new exam, either. Ward knows this because they tried.

Little Ward himself had come up with a plan to repeat the entire school year. "I'll fake an illness," he told his parents, "something that will lay me up for months." He would be a year behind the precious Li Ling, but at least he wouldn't wind up on the dumb-downed, physical-labor education track.

"No room in the class behind Ward's," was the principal's answer when his parents approached the man. "Too many students already in that class."

Overnight, Ward had miraculously recovered from the mysterious illness and returned to school the next morning.

Smile in place, Ward greeted his mother. "Kiel vi, Panjo? I didn't expect you on a Friday."

She held a paperback book in one hand and an orange in the other. Raising an eyebrow, she answered in English. "I'm fine, thank you." Because her own tutor had been British, Panjo spoke with a British accent as did most English speakers her age. The Colony's relationship with the United States was difficult during the first half of the century after the US had interfered in dynastic squabbles, so American tutors in Panjo's generation were rare.

Ward stepped aside to let her enter.

"As for it being Friday, Benny," she continued in English, "they are flushing the septic system in our office building."

Ward knew by the motherly way she was eyeing him that she was seeing if he could follow her foreign words. "I'm happy any day that my mother visits." He folded his arms and smirked. "Won't it be nice to have clean-smelling bathrooms?"

Panjo nodded and offered Ward the fruit. Her smile stretched wide across her broad cheeks. Apparently, he had passed her test. She started to hand him the book, too, but down the hall, a door slammed, and Panjo yelped. She still jumped whenever a car backfired, too. Or when a soldier looked her way.

Ward waited for his mother to regain her composure. She stared unblinking over his shoulder. The seconds ticked by.

To draw her attention, he said, "Panjo, what book is that?"

She was slowly replacing his old books that disappeared during his time at the re-education camp. Her eyes lit up, and she told him it was a Louis L'Amour Western. Ward took it with both hands, pressed it to his chest, flipped the pages, admired the cowboy on the cover, smelled the ink and lignin of the pulp paper, and gently drew his finger along the yellow-painted edges.

Panjo scrunched her face and pointed at the coolie hat leaning up against the nightstand. "Why do you have a peasant hat?"

Ward cleared his throat. "I, well, you know I work outside." He felt as he did when he was fourteen and got caught with a nudie picture the boys at school were passing around.

"But you work at a respectable restaurant. What if someone—"

"No one sees me behind the restaurant working," he said, feeling his true age again, "so I don't mind wearing a peasant hat." He had, in fact, been checking his face in the bathroom mirror every morning, hoping to see his skin getting lighter.

Panjo squeezed her eyes shut. "The restaurant," she said with venom. "American journalists . . ."

Ward set the orange and the book on his desk and turned to face his mother. He knew she often dealt with American press agents. "Journalists? What do you mean, Panjo?"

She waved off his question.

"Panjo, did something happen at work?"

She pursed her lips and said nothing more on the matter. They each had a glass of hot tea, and she left before lunch.

Ward moseyed down to the cafeteria. It wasn't quite noon, and Colony Radio Morning was still on the overhead speakers. Li Ling described minor student protests that were easily handled by troops and not expected to escalate, plus a deadly hornet attack on children. The elementary school at a village in the foothills had sent children "on a field trip to the Northwest Common Forest, and apparently, they disturbed an unusually large nest of great hornets."

The woman in line in front of Ward shook her head. "Stung to death by hornets, what a terrible way to die."

"Colony entomologists have the situation in hand," Li Ling reported, "and the advanced medicine of our Modern Colony will take good care of the survivors of the hornet attack." Her voice was chipper and lyrical in its broadcaster's accent.

"What's an entomologist?" a man at a nearby table said.

Ward spoke up. "Entomologists study insects."

"Every citizen is equal. There are no castes," Li Ling said.

Ward remembered his mother's ancestral icon, how the Great Hornet sat enthroned while the other entities were depicted as small, lowly worshippers. Panjo's own grandparents had migrated from the Blue Mountains, taking their icons and ancestral rituals with them. The all-perfect Great Hornet was the spirit protector of the mountain villages.

Well, that doesn't make sense. If the Great Hornet is a village protector, why were the village children attacked? Ward answered his own question. *Because superstition isn't truth.*

"The Outsiders desire our friendship," Li Ling said on the cafeteria speakers.

Ward picked the pork-squash stir fry.

The way he saw it, people needed a superstition to worship whether it was the Great Hornet or the Bat Gods or some other perfect but untrue god.

"Only drink boiled water," Li Ling said.

Because if people can't choose to worship their perfect superstition, they're left worshipping the imperfect Colony.

Ward's gaze darted around at the diners in the cafeteria. Had anyone guessed what blasphemies he was thinking? He tucked himself into a corner table and ate with his head down, careful not to say anything out loud.

After lunch, Ward settled down once again at his desk to read the newspaper he had found. Turns out it was two days old, and he hadn't realized it this morning when he found it. He folded it up and dropped it in the incinerator and went to look for another paper.

As he passed the bike rack outside the apartment building, he noticed that the boy's new bicycle wore a coat of dust. Holt had given up two months' worth of train tickets so he and Lam could buy the boy a bicycle.

Lam had smiled broadly when she first showed Ward the bicycle. "He begged us for it. He said it'll help him get to and from school faster." She bounced on her toes. "Isn't it wonderful how he's become quite interested in school?"

Ward had been skeptical at the time, and now, seeing the dust, he thought Lam should sell the bicycle.

Ward left the bike rack behind. This time he checked the garbage cans on the other side of Citizens Street.

A tall woman, somewhere in her fifties Ward guessed, hurried past him. She was sobbing and at the same time panting with exertion. She had a pale blue shirt and pristine trousers. A cadre.

Ward quickened his pace to catch her. Perhaps there is something he could do. Ward remembered the thugs who had stolen his sandals. Maybe someone was chasing her. The hairs on the back of his neck rose, and he flexed his arm muscles.

But the restaurant cadre came up a side street, probably on her way to work, and intersected the older woman. They stood shoulder to shoulder on the Citizens Street sidewalk as the older cadre openly cried.

Soon other people joined them on the sidewalk. A young man at the light pole was biting his lip. The woman next to him chewed her fingernails. People hugged themselves and jiggled on nervous feet, everyone looking northward.

Ward stopped too. *What's going on?*

It wasn't long before silence fell over the pedestrian crowd. Cars pulled over. Cyclists stopped and planted a foot on the ground.

A caravan of ancient city ambulances approached. The city was very efficient at repairing older model government vehicles rather than buying new ones.

Four city ambulances went by.

Why aren't they in a hurry? Why aren't the sirens blaring and lights flashing?

More vehicles, small trucks with canvas tarps over the back ends, followed. And finally, a newer model ambulance with Northwest Common Forest Village printed on the side in logograms.

As the last ambulance passed, the older cadre wailed. Her broad cheekbones and narrow-set eyes . . .

Of course. He should have noticed her physical characteristics earlier. She was from the mountain villages. The ambulances and trucks carried her people's children.

Her knees buckled, and Ward rushed to catch her.

The restaurant cadre looked surprised to see him. "Help me keep her upright," she said.

"But she's barely standing," Ward said. "We should let her sit."

"No!" the restaurant cadre screamed. "Keep her on her feet."

The slow-moving ambulances disappeared behind a curve in the road. Cars and bicycles rolled once more. Honks and the *ching-ching* of handlebar bells filled the air. Pedestrians moved, the slap of their plastic shoes on concrete mixing with exclamations of tragedy and sadness for the school children.

The restaurant cadre's sharp voice pierced the murmur of the moving crowd. She shouted something about the Politburo at the older cadre.

The mountain-peasant-cum-cadre squared her shoulders and wiped her face. She straightened her legs for her Colony god and pushed Ward away.

As Ward left the two women, he remembered that a Politburo representative would be visiting the restaurant later that day, not to eat, but to evaluate it, to evaluate the employees, their jobs, Ward's job.

Ward's own knees threatened to buckle.

* * *

Sure enough, as Ward was herding the first of several dogs, the Politburo representative and his entourage toured the restaurant. The representative was a middle-aged, ugly man and had an Outsider's style haircut with his hair parted far to the side of his round head. Fay stood with the entourage in the courtyard. She had placed her hands behind her back and was smiling too big and laughing too much.

"Very good, very good," the Politburo representative said as he scanned the courtyard. The man asked Fay a question.

When she answered, her voice cracked, but she retained her smile, her too big smile.

"You make more money than I do," the representative said, and he laughed, and then his entourage laughed. Everybody laughed except the restaurant cadre. She stood against the glass-topped wall, her eyes narrowing.

Fay's gaze darted to the cadre, and her smile faltered. Ward had no idea if Fay would suffer for whatever code she had apparently breached, but the what-if, the uncertainty of whether or not a cadre would act, put people on edge. It made them guard their words, look over their shoulders, and hide what they were reading. It could be as torturous as an actual punishment.

* * *

The Politburo representative and his entourage weren't the only unusual group to schedule a visit to the restaurant. On a Saturday in May, the cadre gathered employees in the courtyard before work. It had grown unseasonably hot, and smog trapped the heat like a dirty blanket drawn over the city.

A server grumbled that he had to go outside in the early afternoon sun.

The chef wrinkled his nose at Ward. "I don't want a grimy peasant in the kitchen."

Ward tensed. "I'm not a peasant," he said, wishing he hadn't worn his coolie hat that day.

The chef crossed his arms. "Then why —"

"Enough!" yelled Fay. "I don't want Ward tracking blood and feces all over the kitchen, and the butchering room still stinks like chlorine, so here we are. Let's listen to what the cadre has to say."

The cadre leaned forward as if telling them a secret. "Be careful of the group that is to visit sometime in the next week; we don't know exactly when yet. They are Americans," she said in an uncharacteristically low voice. "Their ideas are poisonous. *They* are poisonous, but we must allow them to visit."

A gust of wind blew bits of fur among the group. Ward recognized tufts from last night's collie.

The cadre spat and glared at Fay.

Fay took a step back. "What did I do?"

"If you," said the cadre, now speaking with the assertive voice of a Modern Colonist woman, "hadn't grown the business to such a degree, it wouldn't attract Outsiders."

Fay looked around at the group as if asking for support. "It's a village initiative."

"Ha!" said the cadre. "That's what you'd like people to think, but you have your own agenda."

Fay dropped her gaze.

The cadre pointed at Ward. "And you, start using the water buffalo tool."

The chef stepped forward. "You mean the bolt gun? No, it'll ruin the flavor of my dishes."

Fay shushed him with a wave of her hand. "I think I understand." She looked at the cadre. "The Americans aren't coming because they want to see a successful Colony business, are they?"

The cadre shook her head.

Ward asked, "Then why do we have to let them visit?"

The cadre quoted a tenet that had been broadcast with more frequency lately. "The Outsiders desire our friendship."

Ward didn't care if the bolt gun ruined the flavor of the dishes. He'd never had dog meat, and he never would. For the next several days he walked with a springier step and stood a little taller. The cadre brought in tarps to cover the tops of the cages, shielding the dogs from the sun, and Fay hid Ward's bamboo pole.

* * *

A dozen Americans arrived on a breezy but unrelentingly hot Wednesday afternoon. Ward had seen Outsiders from a distance before, diplomats and journalists entering the building where his mother translated, but never up close, and never Americans, or "Big Noses" as Colonists were apt to call them.

They stomped into the courtyard with angry faces and cameras. The restaurant cadre followed behind them with her lips pressed in a hard, flat line. The Big Noses smelled of cosmetics and sugary soda and were a kaleidoscope of color with hair from straw to black and skin from peach to deep brown. They did, indeed, have big noses, at least compared to the ubiquitous button noses of the Colonists. The group ranged in age from early twenties to Panjo's age. Almost all of them were overweight. Their faces were skewed with emotion, and spit flew as they yelled at Ward.

"Killer!"

"Butcher!"

"Inhumane!"

The dogs backed up to the far corners of their cages, away from the noise of the strangers.

Ward was about to uncage a couple of dogs when one of the Americans, a man with a camera, started circling Ward, taking photos. Ward froze. The wind picked up, swirling dust at their feet.

The cadre lifted her two-way radio to her mouth. Her biceps twitched. She spoke something into her radio then told Ward to carry on with his work.

Ward brushed past the cameraman. Knowing he could use a bolt gun and that it'd be easy to kill a large dog, Ward freed a massive, brown mutt and put a rope around its neck. The Big Noses got louder and stamped their feet and called Ward a killer.

A pale woman with thin, strawberry blonde hair clamped her hand over her mouth and started crying.

"Torturer!" the Big Noses yelled.

Ward let go of the leash while he cocked the bolt gun.

The Big Noses went quiet and looked at each other as if confused. They must not have been expecting a bolt gun. After a moment they resumed their shouts.

The dog slunk to the distant side of the courtyard, and Ward trotted after the animal. Ward pulled on the rope to situate the large dog, and then he placed the bolt gun at the back of the dog's head and pressed the trigger.

The dog dropped, the Big Noses fell silent, and the strawberry blonde woman fainted. Wind quickly drew a curtain of her own hair over her face. Ward stared at the group while they stared at him, and the cadre looked back and forth between the Outsiders and Ward. She planted her feet a little wider, her knees flexed. She looked ready to pounce.

Ward remembered how fast the athletic cadre could move, and he whispered thanks to the ancestors that he was not her target this time.

Suddenly one of the Americans broke from the crowd and ran at Ward. The Big Nose man pulled a plastic bag from within the folds of his shirt. The bag appeared heavy and wobbled with a red fluid inside.

Blood. Ward took a step back, but there was nowhere to go. He was up against the courtyard wall.

A sneer spread across the Big Nose's features.

The cadre took chase.

In a loud voice, Ward said in English, "Yes, I am a murderer," to the charging man.

The man stopped, his mouth agape.

The restaurant cadre likewise paused, and her eyes grew wide. "Ward?" she said. "What . . .?"

Jiggling the liquid-filled bag in his hands, the Big Nose looked back at the crowd and then at the wide-eyed cadre. He seemed to make a decision and launched the bag at Ward and retreated.

The liquid missile flew hard and fast toward Ward. He dodged to the side, but the wind caught the bag and slung it at Ward's throat.

Ward's neck and the front of his shirt were coated in a slick, red fluid that smelled of acrylic. Paint, not blood. The limp body of the brown mutt at Ward's feet was half-covered in paint too.

The Big Noses began yelling again as the cadre herded the paint thrower back to the group. From the back door of the restaurant, two soldiers emerged with AK-47s. The paint-throwing man gathered his unconscious companion, and the soldiers ushered the Americans through the same door and presumably out the front of the restaurant.

"Are you hurt?" the cadre asked as she looked Ward over.

"No."

"Was that English you spoke?"

Ward hadn't felt a rush of fear when the Big Nose ran at him, no adrenaline, nothing. There had been no urge to defend himself, just a desire to avoid being doused with what Ward had thought was blood. In contrast, the cadre made his pulse accelerate and his armpits itch.

Should he lie and tell her it wasn't English, that he had spoken gibberish because he had been afraid?

The breeze was cooling the paint on Ward's neck. He wondered if the cadre could see the paint pulsing with his racing heartbeat.

He wouldn't lie. It was obvious from the Big Noses' reaction that he had spoken English. He hoped his mother wouldn't get in trouble.

"Yes," he finally said.

She nodded slowly, seemingly lost in thought as her rapid breathing from all the ruckus returned to normal.

The paint felt stiff and heavy on his shirt. He shifted his shoulders, and paint dripped onto his pants.

"How many dogs today?" the cadre asked.

Ward was supposed to kill two dogs today, but the mutt on the ground was huge. He pointed to the dead dog. "Just this one."

"Take the dog inside to the butchering room and go home."

* * *

On his way home, Ward alternately splayed and curled his fingers. He was surprised he could feel them. He had stayed within his body. He decided he liked using the bolt gun and didn't feel so much like a killer.

The boy's bicycle was gone. Ward saw the boy sitting on the stoop and leaning over an open box. Ward expected the boy to be upset about the missing bicycle, but the boy looked up at Ward and smiled.

Eyeing Ward's clothes, the youth's smile faded. "Is that blood?" His voice held more curiosity than horror.

"Paint." Ward nodded at the box. "What's in there?"

"Look at this!" The boy rose and held the box out for Ward to see. "I traded my stupid bicycle for a dozen rhino beetles."

"You got rid of your bicycle?" Ward shook his head. Lam could have sold the bicycle and bought some leather sandals.

"It was a defective bicycle. It wobbled all over the place and it made my legs burn."

Ward was about to point out the obvious, that his bicycle was exactly like everyone else's, but an eight-centimeter beetle reached the top of the box and was about to tumble over the edge. Ward nudged the insect back down, and the boy slammed the lid shut.

"I'm going to enter them in fights and get rich."

Ward grimaced but held his tongue. It was refreshing for once to see the boy excited about something even if it was distasteful.

The paint on Ward's clothes was drying fast. He needed to hurry inside and wash them. "Ĝis poste," *Goodbye for now,* he said. He would speak to the boy another time about the value of a bicycle.

That night the Big Noses' angry faces haunted Ward's dreams, and scores of strawberry blonde women lay unconscious in the restaurant's courtyard as if the courtyard itself was paved with bodies. He couldn't catch any dogs without stepping on woman after woman.

By morning, even though he had soaked his shirt and trousers overnight in the little sink in his apartment, the paint still refused to come out. He wrung out his clothes. At least they weren't sticky anymore. He put on the damp, stained clothes, and went down to breakfast.

In the cafeteria, Ward sat next to the boy. He was leaning on his elbow and poking at his rice with his fork.

"What's wrong?" Ward asked.

"I left my fighting beetles together in the box overnight, and they attacked each other. The last surviving beetle is so beat up that it isn't good anymore for fighting."

"Do you miss your bicycle?" Ward asked the youth.

The boy pushed a clump of rice from one side of the bowl to the other and back again. "Yes."

* * *

Later that day, when Ward arrived at work and was untangling the nooses, Fay leaned out the back door and told him the chef needed two dogs. She stared at him for a moment before stepping into the courtyard and plucking at the broad paint stain on his shirt. "Those Americans were just upset because they keep dogs as pets, a luxury. They don't understand." Grinning, she swaggered around like a cowboy and stuck her tummy out. "They don't know hunger. Look how ugly they are."

She paused before him and stood normally. "Ward, I, uh." Her gaze drifted about the courtyard. She plucked his shirt again. "Did you try to wash it out?"

"Yes, but it's stained for good."

"Big Noses," she said with a huff.

Ward stuck his gut out and swaggered around bowlegged like she had done.

One side of Fay's mouth curled up in a half-smile. She held it for a second then turned and went inside.

Ward readied the first noose while he thought about what Fay had said. He wasn't sure she was right about Big Noses not understanding hunger. He'd read plenty of American books that talked about starving times. Every Louis L'Amour book had someone who was hungry. Then there was *A Tree Grows in Brooklyn,* and he'd never forget the struggles of the Joad family in *The Grapes of Wrath.* He wished he still had *The Grapes of Wrath* and hoped his mother would be able to replace it.

No, the Big Noses understand hunger, and they know in their hearts they'd eat their pets if they were hungry enough.

He cocked the bolt gun and let a juvenile mastiff out of its cage.

Also, thought Ward, why did the cadre have him switch to the bolt gun just before the Americans arrived? He knew the answer. Big Noses didn't like beating dogs to death any more than he did. The cadre had simply tried to get ahead of the situation by telling him to use the bolt gun instead. It did seem to confuse the Big Noses for a bit.

"Your life is over," he said as he almost smiled at the mastiff, "but with the bolt gun your death is easier." He pressed the trigger, and the dog dropped.

* * *

After work, when Ward was climbing the stairs in the apartment building, a noise from above caught his attention. It sounded like Lam was hurt. He ran the rest of the way up the stairs and into the third-floor hallway.

Lam's apartment door was open, and her sobs spilled into the hallway.

Ward burst into the apartment.

She was standing before the living room window with her back to him, and her shoulders were shaking. Her son's bedroom door was closed, and the boy was sitting at the desk, scribbling in a textbook. His school-issued composition book lay open and blank.

"Lam, are you okay?"

She turned to face Ward and let out a tearful laugh.

The composition book flew at Ward. He ducked, and the book landed in the hallway.

Lam wiped a glob of snot on her sleeve and gestured at her son. "He doesn't want to do homework."

Ward had the urge to yank the overgrown brat out of his chair and give him a good spanking, but Holt's voice coming from within the bedroom stopped him.

"Is that bastard Ward here?"

Bastard? Oh, no. "Lam, why is Holt home?"

The boy flopped back in his chair. "Patro's hiding in my room because he's in a bad mood."

"Lam?" Ward's mouth went dry.

She motioned for Ward to join her in the hallway, and he followed her. Her hands were trembling. She leaned in and whispered, "He knows. Holt knows about you and me."

* * *

Ward was eighteen when it happened. Lam had recently recovered from her third abortion. It was the middle of the week, late morning, and Holt was in Victory City.

Ward said hello when he encountered her in the apartment hallway. Instead of returning the greeting, Lam tugged on Ward's calloused fingers, pulling him into her apartment. She shut the door.

She smelled of soap and cigarettes back then, and pork and garlic and hot electrical wires, electrical wires because she was still working as a hardware technician. He stood there, not moving deeper into the apartment, not knowing what to do.

"Holt can't make a boy." Her gaze dragged its way around his brawny body and came to rest on his crotch. "I know you could."

His virgin penis reacted.

When she took off her blouse and bra, Ward's gaze zeroed in on her dark nipples. He felt like he should leave, but he didn't want to leave.

She moved forward, kissed him on his lips then his neck. Her kisses felt like soft swipes of a feather and made goosebumps rise on his arms. Then her glossy, unruly locks caressed his cheek, and his hands and lips finally responded. After a moment of confusion when he tried to mount her in the manner of a dog, they made love.

* * *

Ward's bowels turned to liquid upon hearing that Holt had learned their secret. He looked past Lam into the apartment. Holt was at the table now with the boy. They were both hunched over the textbook.

"Does the boy know too?" Ward asked in a whisper.

Lam shook her head no.

Just then the boy yelled, "But why? It's stupid!" He came full speed out of the apartment, and Lam put her arms out as if to embrace her upset child, but the boy shoved her away then shoved her again so hard she cried out and tumbled to the floor.

Ward jumped between the boy and his mother. "If you ever," Ward said, jabbing his finger at the boy, "touch her again, I'll kill you." He immediately regretted it. After all, the boy was his son.

The boy's mouth dropped open, and he backed away from Ward.

Ward stooped to help Lam get up just as Holt came out of the apartment and started punching the boy about his bulbous face and neck. The boy looked stunned, and then he started dodging the blows with the quick reflexes of a youth. Holt continued to swing, only occasionally landing on an ear, a shirt collar, a wisp of hair.

Lam begged her husband to stop.

The boy's stunned expression had morphed into a red ball of anger. When the boy clenched his fists, Ward quickly hooked his hand around Holt's shoulder and pulled him away from the boy's reach.

"Holt, stop," Ward said. "This is not the right way."

The diminutive man kept lashing out, wildly swinging at air.

"Before the cadre comes," Ward added.

Holt spun and punched Ward in the ribs. Ward remained in place, unaffected by the blow, but Holt stumbled back, cradling his fist.

The four Colonists grew still, the boy now clinging to his mother, Lam with her eyes cast down, Holt clutching his hand and glaring at his wife, and Ward staring at his son.

Finally, the boy broke the silence. He pushed away from his mother. "I hate you. I hate school." Tears dripped from his pudgy cheeks. "I hate everything!" He ran into the apartment, and a moment later, his bedroom door slammed.

Ward shuffled down the hall to his apartment.

* * *

Holt's discovery of the boy's paternity and the drama in the hallway ate away at Ward throughout the night and into Friday morning. In the cafeteria, even Li Ling's entrancing delivery of the news that's significant to the citizens—*Gorbachev arrived in the Colony yesterday and met with senior Colony officials, including the Chairman*—failed to put Ward's mind at ease.

He walked to work with his head down, replaying the hallway scene over and over again. In the courtyard, when he accidentally smacked his head on the slaughter frame, Fay left the bucket she was filling, marched over, and grabbed his arm.

"Are you still upset because of the Americans? You snap out of it! Leave those Americans out of your thoughts." She let go of his arm with a push.

"It's not about that," he said. "My neighbor—"

"Because we have a very important customer coming next week," Fay said, ignoring him. "She has reservations exactly one week from tonight. Big money." She poked him in the chest. "You must be perfect." As she spoke, her face softened. She cleared her throat. "Not just you, *everything* must be perfect." She grabbed her bucket and went inside.

Fay popped her head out a moment later with the bamboo pole. "Now that the Outsiders are gone and for certain aren't coming back, you will go back to the proper way of dispatching the dogs."

His right hand went numb as soon as he took the pole from Fay.

Ward killed three dogs that afternoon. The respite he'd had while using the bolt gun meant his hands had softened somewhat. As he struck the third dog, blood from newly formed blisters added to the canine blood at his feet.

He couldn't feel his blistered hands, of course.

When Ward took the carcasses inside, he found Fay in the butchering room, sharpening the chef's knives. The rasping noise was normally like bits of glass grinding his eardrums, but he had yet to return to his body, so the noise didn't bother him. She gave him a quick nod. "You were fast. Very good."

"Who is the important person coming next week?" Ward asked as his mind suddenly slid into his body, and he hung the dogs upside down over the drain for the chef. "A politician, a celebrity?"

Each rhythmic *scritch-scritch* on the honing steel now sent thorny shivers down his spine. He shouldn't have asked any questions. He should have just hung the dogs and gotten out of there.

Scritch-scritch.

Fay laid down the knife and honing steel. "You won't believe who it is. I can hardly believe she's coming *here*, to the Yulin Dish, to my restaurant." She rubbed her hands together and grinned. "Li Ling!"

* * *

Ward passed through the days leading up to Li Ling's dinner party in a blur. Meals at the cafeteria, newspaper foraging, uncomfortable glances at Lam, views looking down on the top of his head as he worked, washing canine blood from his clothes, more meals at the cafeteria, newspapers, Lam, the top of his head, canine blood.

At last, the day of Li Ling's party arrived. Ward changed his typical, stained shirt for the clean shirt he reserved for his mother's visits. He left his peasant hat in his apartment.

Walking to the restaurant, Ward practiced scenarios in his mind.

Kiel vi, maljuna amiko? he'd say.

Her eyes would flash. *"Old friend"? Ward, we're not old.* She'd laugh, and her cheeks would turn pink like before. *We're in the prime of our life!*

Or maybe she'd approach him first, kiss him on the cheeks in the scandalous way the Europeans are said to do. Being a celebrity, she could get away with it.

I've missed you, Ward, she'd say after kissing him. She wouldn't step back. She'd be standing closer than necessary.

It's good to see you, Li Ling, he'd say. He wouldn't step back, either.

When Ward arrived at the restaurant, Fay told him Li Ling's dinner party required four kills. Ward scanned the courtyard. There were exactly four dogs in the cages, two hounds that had been there a week, and two new dogs, a husky female, and a long-haired retriever. Four would take a long time, a husky making it even longer, but he had no choice.

He opened the cages. The hounds explored the courtyard, nose-to-concrete. The husky leaped toward freedom, but when Ward moved to block her, she dodged left when she should have gone right. He easily slipped the noose over her head.

After Ward had ropes around all four dogs, he secured them in the slaughtering frame, lifted the bar into place, and picked up the stained pole. The dogs struggled, kicked at the air, ran in place, and slavered. None of them were heavy enough to pull the noose tight and asphyxiate themselves. They'd have slow, painful deaths. He paused a moment as his mind slipped away from his body, and then he started in on the husky. If he left her for last, he might not have enough strength to finish the job.

Over the next hour, he watched himself work on the writhing dog. He delivered precision strikes that landed only on soft tissue or large joints, never the head or spine. The husky's back arched as she cried out. Her midsection became flaccid as her abdominal muscles and internal organs broke apart. She'd be bleeding inside, and that, in turn, would slow her nervous system's responses. At one point a mass of blood and lumps fell to the ground beneath her. It was not unusual for dogs to defecate and urinate as their bodies shut down, sometimes with blood emerging, too, from the internal wounds.

She screamed and yelped until her voice gave out, and then there was nothing but silent spasms. She bared her teeth with each strike. One of her eyes dilated. Blood seeped through the skin on her belly where her fur wasn't as thick, and the sounds of Ward's assault turned to grotesque spatter noises. A minute later her spasms ceased, and a minute after that her breathing ceased, too.

Panting from his exertion, Ward dropped his arms and backed up. As he looked down to avoid stepping on the pile of blood and feces that had fallen from the husky's dying body, he saw five mounds of flesh. Not feces, but puppies. She had been pregnant. They were hairless, partially formed, and blue, and they had bulging orbs where their eyes should be—or would have been if given a chance.

One of the puppies stirred, and it arched its back as its mother had done. *To fall from the warm softness and heartbeat lullaby of its mother's womb to the hard silence of the concrete!* Ward's thinking self, hovering somewhere above his head, was surprised to see his corporeal self weeping. He had never cried for the dogs before.

He quickly stomped on the puppy's head to release the wretched creature from its pain.

Then he vomited, something else he had never done before.

He wiped away his tears with the back of a bloody hand and turned to the retriever. A breeze had begun to blow, ruffling the retriever's long locks. The dog's eyes were trained on the limp husky. It was rare to see the whites of a dog's eyes unless it was very scared. Ward could see complete, white halos around the retriever's brown irises.

* * *

After the fourth dog succumbed, Ward released the bar and lowered the dogs to the ground. He carried Li Ling's dinner inside to the butchering room and helped the chef position the carcasses on the hooks.

Ward's mind slammed back into his body, and he heard the cheers and laughter of a crowd.

Often the bigger dinner parties had cocktail hours beforehand with much fanfare and handshakes and speeches. When the chef's back was turned, Ward quietly approached the kitchen door and peered in. The far door, the one that led to the dining room, was propped open. If he leaned just right, he could see through the kitchen and into the dining area.

Customers stood in groups of two and three, holding drinks. As a whole, people were turned more or less toward a woman who spoke with broad gestures, her voice a bell.

Li Ling! Ward listened for a moment but couldn't catch her words. Frustrated, he snuck all the way into the kitchen and stood just inside the far door.

"Three members of the Politburo," she was saying, "and none of them knew which version of the story I should report!"

Her audience laughed, and she smiled as her gaze moved about the room.

She made eye contact with Ward where he stood in the doorway.

He drew a breath. His heart danced. His mind struggled to remember what it was that he had planned to say after all this time. *I'm proud of you, I miss you, remember when we . . . my old friend.* "Maljuna amiko," he whispered.

But there was no recognition in her eyes. Her gaze moved on. "If you thought that was funny," she said to her people, "you should hear about the time the Chairman . . ."

"Li Ling!" he called. He took a step into the dining room, and two cadres Ward had never seen before immediately blocked his way.

"Get out of here, peasant," a blue-shirted man said with a growl.

"Li Ling!" Ward called again. He waved.

She briefly turned his direction, her gaze brushing past Ward and returning to her audience. She pivoted her shoulders away from the apparent distraction at the kitchen.

Ward quit waving. He felt the muscles in his face and shoulders go limp. "Li Ling?" he whispered.

The two cadres shoved Ward back into the kitchen and closed the door.

Ward shuffled through the kitchen and into the butchering room, the laughter from Li Ling's party following him like a shadow he couldn't shake. The chef, who was bleeding the dogs, yelled something at Ward, but he didn't hear it. He splashed through the blood and stumbled out to the courtyard.

In a daze, Ward managed to hose down the courtyard for Fay. He knew she'd have her hands full tonight.

It was almost evening when Ward headed home. As he passed

through the alleyway behind the restaurant, he looked down and was surprised to see he had his hand wrapped around the slaughtering pole and was dragging it behind him. It had aged with time, turning from bamboo-gold to tired gray, and splinters blossomed at each frayed end. The day's gentle breeze picked up and tossed about sooty-yellow dust and litter. By the time he approached the apartment building, years' worth of dog matter clinging to the pole was crusted over with the dusty filth of the city.

The boy was sitting on the concrete stairs again, forcing other residents to step around him as they entered and exited. He was picking apart a plastic market basket, a pink one like his mother carried. It probably was his mother's.

"Why do you have your pole?" the boy asked.

Ward shrugged. "I know now that it's a part of me."

The boy rolled his eyes. "You don't make any sense."

"And you look upset."

The boy cussed. "I got my placement exam scores today." He grabbed both sides of the pink market basket, growled, and tore it in two.

"Well?"

"My scores were bad. My classmate says I'll only be good for pushing people onto a bus before the door closes. He says they do that in the really big cities."

Ward nodded. "Bus packers." He leaned on the slaughtering pole and thought of something else the boy would be good at.

Ward recalled his own placement exam and felt a small bubble of compassion for the boy. "Were you sick when you took the exam?"

"No."

The bubble popped.

"Then your classmate is right," Ward said.

The boy jumped up and rushed Ward.

Ward sidestepped and hooked the boy's foot with the pole. The boy's giant mass tumbled to the sidewalk. Ward thought of the money he had saved in the tin box. He finally knew what to do with it.

"I have a job for you," Ward said, looking down at his offspring.

"What job?" the boy asked. He grunted and struggled to his feet.

"Wait here." Ward fetched the money, and then father and son headed toward the train tracks with the tin box and the pole.

"What job?" the boy asked again. "Why are we bringing the pole?" He was panting in his effort to keep up with Ward.

They arrived at the tracks where the alder brush encroached upon the rails. A full-on storm was approaching now, and a blast of wind pushed Ward and his son toward the dark tunnel.

Ward tucked the tin box under an alder. "There are twenty-nine dolaroj in the box."

The boy eyed the box. He licked his lips.

Ward handed his son the pole. "Beat me with the pole. Kill me."

"I'll get caught."

You should have said it's wrong, Son. You should have said no.

A gust yanked the boy's hair from his ugly forehead. A leaf slapped his face.

"The sun is setting." Ward raised his voice above the wind. "Nobody will see you. I'll lie down on the tracks, and afterward, you can leave my body there. People will think the train killed me, that it was a suicide. Then drop the pole over the wall at the Yulin Dish on your way home."

The boy said nothing, so Ward went ahead and lay across the tracks as he had before, his ankles resting on one rail and his neck on the other.

He waited.

Tilting his head as if in thought, the boy eyed the pole and then looked back at the bush where the tin of money hid.

A truck rumbled over the bridge.

The boy gripped the pole in both hands, stood over Ward, and swung the pole downward onto Ward's chest, and again, and again, tentatively at first, but then his blows grew in strength and ferocity.

Ward laughed.

The boy stopped. "What is it?" he shouted. "Why are you laughing?"

"My name," Ward said. "Kalb. It also means *dog*. I am a dog."

"Stop laughing. You're slowing me down." The boy slammed Ward's stomach with the pole, then struck Ward's arms and chest. Drops of blood scattered in the wind and disappeared in the darkening shadows.

Ward felt a rib break, and he smiled at the blissful pain in his chest. Such glorious, living pain.

The boy stopped again. "What now? Why are you smiling?"

"You're doing a good job." The wind was howling through the tunnel now, and with a broken rib it hurt to yell above the noise, but Ward relished that pain, too.

"It's not right that you're smiling. I don't like it." The boy swung again, aiming at Ward's mouth and this time leaning his heft into the blow.

The impact drove Ward's neck against the rail. He felt his vertebrae shift, and his mandible jerked sideways. He had forgotten to tell the boy to avoid the head and spine. "Don't aim for—" His words came out in meaningless vocalizations. He couldn't form words. His tongue and lips wouldn't respond, and what sound did come out of his throat was without force. The boy swung again, this time with a gross leer, aiming at Ward's crotch. Ward went to raise his hand, to show the boy the proper spots to hit, but his arm refused to move. In fact, he felt nothing below his nose.

As the boy continued his assault on Ward's pain-free groin . . . ribs . . . knees, Ward remained helpless. His only ability to communicate was with his eyes. He squeezed his eyes shut then opened them wide. He blinked rapidly.

Look at my eyes, Son, my eyes, my eyes! I can't feel anything except on my head. Jab me in the nose! Strike me in the ear!

The boy's face gleamed red with sweat, effort, and the setting sun as he mangled Ward's thighs and pulverized his belly. Ward yelled to catch his son's attention, and only a weak moan emerged.

The tunnel howled.

The boy continued.

Ward lay disappointed, waiting to die.

END

ACKNOWLEDGEMENTS

A big thanks to the hubster for his constant support. (Let's order pizza!) Thanks also to the talented Loren Rhoads for sharing her writing wisdom, and to my childhood swim coach, Rob VanSlyke, who took eleven-year-old me seriously when I said I wanted to be a writer. Thank you, River Dixon and team, for welcoming me to Potter's Grove Press.

Finally, thanks to YOU, dear reader, for reading my story. Please consider leaving a review on your favorite platform. Reviews help other readers, and the feedback helps me become a better writer.

ABOUT THE AUTHOR

Priscilla Bettis read her first horror story, *The Exorcist*, when she was a little kid. She snuck the book from her parents' den, and *The Exorcist* scared her silly. From that moment on, Priscilla was hooked on horror and all things deliciously off-kilter. As an adult, she turned to engineering physics, a wonderful profession, but what she really likes to do is write. Priscilla is an excellent swimmer, which is good because vampires are terrible swimmers. Priscilla shares a home in the Northern Plains of Texas with her two-legged and four-legged family members.

Website:
priscillabettisauthor.com

Amazon author page:
amazon.com/Priscilla-Bettis/e/B08R97Z63M

Twitter:
@PriscillaBettis

Made in the USA
Coppell, TX
07 November 2022

85938703R00069